RUNNING BACK

Wilburn caught the kick, into top gear, legs poun starting to move him away from the Elmstead coverage. But Jimmy kept his cool, not committing himself too early to the faster runner. He timed his tackle perfectly, angling his body so that he caught the Downham 83 below the knees with his shoulder. Will Thomas was flipped clear into the air in a punishing somersault but just managed to hang on to the football.

'Good tackle, son!' called Jerry Meredith.

From the other side of the field came the bellowing voice of the Downham Coach, Tom Nickleby. 'Wrong, Jerry. Not a good tackle! A *great* tackle!'

Also available from Magnet Books, by the same authors:

The Gridiron Series:

First And Ten
Second And Five
Third And Goal
Touchdown!

And the Baseball series:

Home Run
Grand Slam

Laurence and Matthew James

Running Back

A Magnet Book

This is for Rosanna Nissen, for her successful efforts in spreading the good word. With thanks from both of us.

First published as a Magnet paperback original 1988
by Methuen Children's Books
a division of OPG Services Ltd
Michelin House, 81 Fulham Road, London SW3 6RB
Copyright © 1988, Laurence James.
Printed and bound in Great Britain
by

ISBN 0 416 12192 6

1

'It's make or break time for the San Diego Chargers. Four points behind and only six seconds remaining on the clock in the fourth quarter in this greatest of all Superbowls. The Forty-Niners' defence lined back, waiting for the deep "Hail Mary" pass. But will veteran quarter-back Dan Fouts, with his injured shoulder, dare to throw it? Second and fifteen on the Forty-Niners' thirty-six yard line. The dazzling young English running back, Jimmy Marvin, comes out of the huddle with Fouts. Jimmy already has two touchdowns to his credit this game. Can he make it a hat trick? For this stocky running back, nothing is impossible. Any thoughts, John Madden? The Hail Mary?'

'Not with Dan Fouts' arm being under-strength. I'd fake the deep pass, and slip it to Jimmy. Let the Pocket Thunderbolt try and explode just one more time for it.'

Like so often, Big John had read the game and the play correctly.

Jimmy crouched, oblivious to the searing noise of the huge crowd filling the Dome. The signal had come in from Coach Al Saunders. The words still blazed in Jimmy Marvin's brain, 'Go for it, son. For your

5

family, your country, your team . . . and for me. One last big run.'

In front of him Dan Fouts was stooped, ready for the snap. Counting off, his voice cracked with the bedlam around him. He straightened the leather ball in his capable hands. The receivers were haring off to the right, heading for the end-zone. The defence of the Forty-Niners were running to cover them. Jimmy's eye was caught for a moment by the imposing figure of Ronnie Lott, the six-foot-tall free safety for the San Francisco team. Ronnie wasn't falling back like the others. In the shadows of his helmet, his eyes glittered at Jimmy. And he was half-grinning, like he'd already guessed the play and was just waiting for the young English player to come running smack into his waiting tackle.

Dan feinted the throw, starting to cut to his right, while Jimmy closed in on him. Taking the hand-off of the ball he cradled it to him. He felt his cleats digging into the artificial turf as he powered left, evading the despairing tackle of one of the Forty-Niners' defensive line.

Then he heard the noise.

Thirty-five yards to run. In training they'd timed his speed over forty yards at four point five seconds. Seeing that they'd been wrong-footed, most of the San Francisco defence were already beginning to move back towards the left . . . towards where Jimmy Marvin was running, knees high, his free arm pumping.

Across the thirty.

6

Ronnie Lott, driving in towards him, was like a great hunting shark. But Jimmy was too fast, too elusive for the free safety, dodging around him, feeling the despairing hand brush his ankle.

Across the twenty.

More defenders came towards him, seeing the danger to the line. The roaring from the tiers of seats was deafening. His own name, shouted over and over again, swelling like the waves on rocks, 'Jimmy! Jimmy!! Jimmy!!!'

Another tackle loomed in from his right. He pivoted, half-handing off the San Francisco player, dancing in a circle and leaving the man on the turf.

Across the ten.

One more man to beat. One red jersey between Jimmy Marvin and Superbowl glory.

Out of the corner of his eye the English boy saw one of his own San Diego team throw a block to remove another potential threat to him. One man to beat. Jimmy tensed himself for a last jinking whirl, and then the dive into the end-zone for the winning score.

Five yards.

Now!

'Watch where you're goin', you little idiot! You nearly 'ad me over!'

The querulous voice, coming out of the blackness, ripped Jimmy into the real world, away from the fantasy of winning the Superbowl. Back to the damp streets of Hither Green, in South-East London.

'I'm an OAP, you daft little bleeder! I done me bit

for King an' country and you come runnin' and dodgin' round the bleedin' lampposts like you're Stanley bleedin' Matthews hisself.'

'Sorry,' panted Jimmy, hoisting the bag with his kit in it on to his shoulder. Seeing the old man he'd nearly sent flying Jimmy realised that he knew him and hoped that he hadn't been recognised. But the eyes behind the pebble-thick glasses were sharp as a ferret's peering at him in the pool of silver light from the street-lamp.

'Just a jiff! I know you, don't I? Just 'ang on! It's Jimmy Marvin. I see your Gran down the launderette of a Friday when it's cheap rate for us old ones.'

'Oh, yeah. It's Mr Rowe, isn't it? I'm ever so sorry. I never saw you. I was sort of . . .' The words faded away down the windswept suburban street. The old man didn't look as if he was ready to be mollified yet.

'You was *sort of* not lookin' where you was goin', that's what. Still . . . I suppose you was pretendin' to be one of the Millwall lads, or is it Charlton you support? I come from North London, so it's always been the good old Spurs for me.' He looked at the boy critically, his head on one side. 'Bit short for a soccer player, ain't you, Jimmy? How old are you?'

'Thirteen. And I'm not that short. I'm four-feet six-and-a-half inches.' He knew that because he measured himself every single evening against the door of the bedroom he shared with his adopted older brother, Chris.

'Never mind.' Now Mr Rowe was easing off the pedal. He'd let off steam for the shock the kid had given him, dodging out of the blackness like that. 'You been to soccer trainin', 'ave you?'

'No. No, I play American Football. Not soccer at all.'

'You what?'

'Not soccer. I play American Football. I'm what they call a running back. I was imagining that I was playing for . . .' and then changing his mind. 'Just sort of practising swerving round the lampposts. Sorry.'

'Yank football! Cor blimey!' The old man actually spat across the pavement, into the gutter. 'I never 'eard the like. Fancy a kid like you playin' that nancy game 'stead of soccer! What's the bleedin' world comin' to, eh?' he asked addressing his question to the overcast night sky.

'It's a good game, Mr Rowe. Honest. I bet you never watched it.'

'Never want to watch it, son, and that's the God's own truth. Yank football! 'Ere, wait a minute. Your old man's a Yank, inne?'

'Yeah, Dad was born in the States. But he's lived over here for nearly twenty years.'

'Still a Yank! Any road, I got to get on 'ome. You take care, you 'ear me, Jimmy Marvin.' He turned and began to walk slowly away, towards the station. Jimmy noticed that the old man limped and wore a built-up shoe on his right foot. And he was huddled in a patched overcoat, even though it was a mild July evening. A small van drove noisily by, and as it disappeared, Jimmy could just hear Mr Rowe, still muttering to himself. 'I dunno. Yank football! What's

9

wrong with lads these days? Like everything, I suppose, with all the . . .'

Fading into the stillness.

The excitement and involvement of gridiron training was one of the best moments of the week for Jimmy Marvin. Though school was over and he was on holiday, it wasn't a good time. He was still the best part of a half mile away from home and he started to jog, the bag bouncing against his back. It had rained towards the end of training, breaking three weeks of drought. Hardly enough to moisten the dry earth, but enough to leave a greasy film on the streets and pavements. The boy began to dodge in and out of the lamps, struggling to slip again into his Superbowl dream, but the encounter with old Mr Rowe had broken the spell and soured the sweetness of the fantasy.

In the end he broke off and walked the rest of the way. Reaching the edge of the sprawling council estate just after half-past nine. He stopped at the front gate, seeing through the undrawn curtains that his parents were sitting either side of the fireplace, talking animatedly. Jimmy hoped that they weren't having another of their rows.

'Home, sweet home,' he said.

Home was a three bedroomed, end of terrace house in crumbling white stucco with metal-framed bay windows at the front. It had once been a part of a show council estate, but time had taken its toll. Now the corner where Jimmy Marvin and his family lived was depressingly run down and neglected.

When it rained the water dribbled from a cracked gutter, splashing on the porch over the front door. The windows at the back were warped and let in draughts in winter and couldn't be opened properly even in the heat of summer. A small, dank river ran along the backs of the houses, where everyone threw their rubbish. Old prams and rotting mattresses sometimes blocked it so that the spring rains made the gardens flood. You also saw rats scurrying under the red brick arches.

The Marvins had lived down near Hither Green for about three years. Jimmy couldn't rightly recall all of their other homes, but he was sure that this one was the pits. Every time they moved it seemed to him that the buildings got smaller and scruffier and the surroundings less pleasant.

Before this house there'd been three other council houses, all quite close together. One had been further along the Dartford Loop Line into Charing Cross. That had been nice, with a big garden and fields close at hand. And there'd been four bedrooms, so Jimmy hadn't needed to share with Chris.

Now things were different.

Mum and Dad slept at the front of the house, Jimmy and his older brother in the larger room at the back, not far from the clattering of the railway, and seventeen-year-old Kate, his sister, had the box-room at the back. Which she'd filled with pictures of her favourite actors, singers and groups – Emilio Estevez and Matt Dillon, New Order and The Smiths. And there was a huge anti-fur poster that always made Jimmy feel a bit sick when he saw it, even though he agreed with her that wearing the skins of dead animals was horrible.

Kate worked in a department store in Lewisham and had a steady boyfriend called Roger. Both Chris and Jimmy thought that Roger was a bit of a drip, but Mum and Dad liked him. They said he was 'quiet' and 'reliable'. Jimmy wondered whether those were virtues that would get you on in life. All the adults seemed to think so, but he wasn't convinced.

The walls of the big rear bedroom were plagued with condensation, and streamed with damp in cold weather, despite all of Mum's efforts with an old paraffin heater. Black mould grew in the corners and if you weren't careful it got on your clothes. Posters tended to rot and fall down within days, but both boys still kept trying to stick pictures up.

Jimmy's pictures were mainly of American footballers. Some of his greatest heroes. Pride of place went to the stocky running back from the San Diego Chargers. Number twenty-six, Lionel James was known as 'Little Train' for the way he would steam through opposition tacklers, flattening men twice his size. There was also a nice action poster of the San Diego veteran quarter-back, Dan Fouts, hurling off a touchdown pass.

Just as Jimmy was a bit on the short side for his age, so Chris Marvin was very tall and powerful for fifteen. He played rugby for whatever school he happened to be attending and had also represented area Colts XVs, generally at lock in the middle of the back row of the scrum. A year ago he'd become infected by Jimmy's enthusiasm for the gridiron game and now played outside linebacker for the Under Seventeen squad of the Elmstead Victors. Jimmy was in the Under Fourteens. Chris's favourite poster was a terrifying photo of the New England Patriots' number fifty-six charging through for a tackle. Pro-Bowler André Tippett.

The furniture in the bedroom was rickety, though Dad had painted it a year ago, trying to brighten it up. There were two bunk beds, too short for Chris's six-feet-two, a wardrobe with only one door and a large table with a scarred top where they both did their homework. There was a bookshelf on one wall which housed Jimmy's prized collection of Stephen King books. Nearly a complete set, from *Carrie* right through to *The Tommyknockers*.

The only luxury in the room was a third-hand stack system. Both boys liked music, despite having different tastes. Chris had been dead keen on reggae for a couple of years, but was now moving into heavy metal, much to Jimmy's disgust. His love was early Motown records by performers like Stevie Wonder, The Supremes, Martha Reeves, The Four Tops, The Temptations and Smokey Robinson.

Two years earlier, in one of the Marvin family's rare strokes of luck, one of Mum's five premium bonds had come up with two hundred and fifty pounds. After some outstanding debts had been settled, there was enough for each child to have a wondrous fifty pounds. Jimmy blew his on a boxed set of nine albums, called 'Motown Chartbusters . . . 150 Hits Of Gold'. It was probably his most treasured possession. The Marvins weren't too great on possessions.

Jimmy paused in the tiny front garden, and peered in, unseen, at his parents.

His father looked tired, slumped in the armchair with the broken springs. Even at thirteen, Jimmy was more than aware that all wasn't well. His parents had been married for nineteen years now and Dad had left America to settle in London. He was a skilled plumber and for the first twelve years or so everything fine. What Dad called 'hunky-dory'. Trying to carry a heavy immersion heater up a makeshift ladder into a loft in Willesden, he'd fallen. Four months in hospital with crushed vertebrae . . . Jimmy remembered the phrase. He also remembered something about 'unadequate insurance'.

Sometimes Jimmy tried to look back and see the milestones marking the slow, inexorable downhill path. There'd been the odd feeling that friends from school gradually seemed to be living in nicer houses than his. His mates had good bikes. Most had a BMX, but Dad couldn't afford one. Same when skateboards made a big come-back.

Even American Football was the same. When Jimmy started getting interested in the game, encouraged by his father, watching it on Channel Four, buying the kit had been a big problem. And when Chris took the game up as well, joining the Elmstead Victors and playing a year above his age, the big problem became almost insurmountable. Fortunately for Chris, Elmstead were allied to an adult gridiron team and they were able to get a helmet and shoulder-pads from one of the men who was packing the game in. But when you were only four-and-a-half feet tall, plus the odd half inch or so, then it was really difficult.

Jimmy hefted his bag on to his shoulder again, feeling where the broken and knotted strap dug into his sore skin. Dad had managed to get a part-time job, six months ago, until they discovered how bad his back was and fired him. During that time there'd been a few pounds more than usual coming in and the battered football helmet had been a snip at ten pounds. The club provided the pants and playing shirts, and a pair of old soccer boots from the Oxfam shop in Lewisham finished off Jimmy's rag and tag outfit.

The garage at the side of the house stood empty, one door off its hinges. Jimmy could just remember, when he'd been younger, that they'd owned a car. A pale green saloon with a gear-box that was always giving Dad hassle. Now they took the train or the bus. Jimmy was used to it and didn't really mind. The only time it was embarrassing was when the team were playing away and he had to scrounge a lift from one of the other boys.

He opened the back door and crept into the kitchen. Jimmy had learned years ago that it wasn't a good idea with other boys, until he knew and could trust them, to let on that his father did the cooking in their home. Not just every other Friday, but virtually all the meals they had. Some kids thought it was a big laugh. 'Soft, is he, your Dad?' they'd say. 'You gonna wear a pretty apron like your old man, Jimmy?' they'd tease.

Truth was, Burgess Marvin, born on the Lower East Side of New York, loved cooking. During the last few depressing years, Jimmy had often heard his father say that cooking was the only thing that kept him going.

Despite being American, Burge was the world's number one fan of English food. In the kitchen was a big shelf, crowded with cookery books. *Fine British Fare* jostled *The Roaste Beef of Olde Englande*. A well-thumbed copy of *Traditional Dishes of Cornwall* leaned for support against an almost mint paperback called
16

Dandelion and Burdock in Meat Braising. Dad admitted that it was one of his mistakes, but he still wouldn't throw it away.

Jimmy stood for a minute in the kitchen, sniffing the air, trying to guess what supper had been. Training had lasted over two hours and before it Dad had whipped up a fluffy omelette with strips of bacon and some crisp fried bread for him. The evening meal for the others smelled like it had been some sort of grilled meat. Maybe lamb? Dad was fond of lamb. And there were the stalks of some mushrooms in the rubbish dish by the sink.

Down the hall, through the half-open door, the boy could hear his parents' voices, raised in an edgy conversation. Not a row or anything, but he could almost taste the tension in the air.

Jimmy sighed.

'I'm not sure, love.' That was Beth Marvin, sounding tired. Not wanting to argue with her husband.

'But all these new rules and stuff, honey. This guy Baker's gotten his way and it looks like curtains for sociology teachers like you.'

'It's not definite.'

Jimmy froze, half-way along the hall, not wanting to walk in on them and not wanting them to know he'd been eavesdropping on their talk. It sounded like bad news. Mum was a teacher at one of the comps up towards Eltham. A sociology teacher. She'd found it harder over the years, as they moved around the city, to get a new job. And now . . . if she was out of work again, then . . .?

'Oh, God! I keep lookin' out for the light at the end of the railroad tunnel, Beth. And it keeps turning out to be a train coming in the wrong direction. If only my back wasn't . . .' His father said something else, his voice dropping so that his listening son couldn't quite catch it. His mother also spoke, but he couldn't hear what she was saying.

Then it was Burge Marvin again: 'We're already in Debt City, USA, love. A long way down on Desolation Row.'

Jimmy had never heard his dad sounding so depressed. His voice broke, almost as if he was going to cry.

'Oh, love,' said Mum, comfortingly. The same kind of voice she used if Jimmy or Chris had fallen over and scraped a knee or an elbow.

Jimmy started to turn round, deciding he'd go in the kitchen and make himself a cup of tea. Give things time to settle down before he went into the living-room. When he heard a door open upstairs and a burst of what might have been Whitesnake. Chris's voice floated down over the bannisters, calling to their mother.

'Did you wash my playing-shirt, Mum? Got training tomorrow.'

Jimmy spun on his heel and darted silently into the kitchen. Easing open the back door.

'Machine's packed in again, Chris. Dad washed it by hand. It's still out on the line.'

'But it's raining, innit? Jimmy back yet? Ask him to get it in, Mum.'

Jimmy banged the back door shut. 'Get your own shirt. It's not raining much, anyway.'

'Oh, go on. I've got nothin' on me feet, Jimmy. Please.'

'No. I'm in now.' He paused. 'And you better turn off that Motorhead. I got some English homework I got to do.'

'It's not Motorhead, you dimlow! It's Whitesnake! Mum!' Trying a last appeal.

Beth Marvin came out into the hall. Jimmy thought her eyes looked a bit red, but he didn't say anything. That was something else he'd learned over the years.

'Hello, Mum.'

'Hi, Jim. How did training go?'

'All right. I bumped into Mr Rowe on the way home.'

'Oh, the old boy that Gran sees at the launderette. She reckons he's after her.'

Gran was Beth's mother, who lived only a few streets away in a little terraced house close by the station in Leahurst Road. She'd lived there on her own since her husband, Mum's father, had died of a heart attack on Coronation Day in 1953. 'He laughed too much at that big fat Queen of Tonga. Went out 'Pop' like a light bulb blowin'. Spoilt the street party, it did.' Though he thought it was vaguely shocking, Jimmy loved to hear his Gran tell the story. She was always chewing Fox's Glacier Mints and the house was full of little bits of blue and white wrapping paper.

'Want a cuppa, Jim?'

'Please, Mum. Thanks.'

'Make us one, Mum!' yelled Chris, from half-way up the stairs.

'Please,' prompted Dad, emerging into the hall, rubbing the small of his back like he did whenever he had been sitting still in one place for too long a time.

'All right. Jim. Go and get your brother's team shirt in off the line, will you?'

'OK.'

As he started to open the door, his father came through into the kitchen. 'Training all right, son?' he asked.

'Sure. Worked on some plays for the charity game next week.'

'Against the Downham Destroyers from up the M Eleven?'

'Yeah. It's for the local hospital scanner. Our coach, Jerry Meredith, knew their coach back in the States. They're supposed to be well crucial. Got a great quarterback and a wide receiver, and they've been in the gridiron papers, Coach says.'

Chris leaned on his father's shoulder, grinning at his younger brother. 'Don't forget you got me an' a half-dozen of the Under Seventeens in the game. We'll wipe 'em away for you.'

Jimmy grinned back. Suddenly the kitchen was crowded. All it needed was his sister, but Kate would be out with her boyfriend at this time of night. Jimmy felt his earlier sadness lifting. Sure, a lot of his mates had bigger and nicer houses, but there weren't many of them that had the great feeling of warmth and love that was set loose in his home.

That night, in bed, Jimmy and Chris talked about their parents' current problems. The older boy had also overheard their earlier conversation.

'I was ear-holing on the landing when I heard you come creepin' in the back. But it looks like Mum might lose her job. Be real bad, if that happened. We'd only have the Social and what Kate brings in. I reckon I might leave school, Jimmy. Try and get a job some place.'

'But you got your A Levels.'

'Money gets you through times of no A Levels better than A Levels gets you through times of no money,' said Chris.

'I could get another paper round,' tried Jimmy. 'Get up earlier and fit one in for Mr Patel in the other newsagents.'

'You're up at six already. Don't be a sap, brother. Maybe the school won't kick Mum out.'

'If only Dad could get a real cool job doing cooking. His back wouldn't stop him doing that.'

Chris's voice floated from the other bunk. 'Pigs might fly, Jim. You know how many times he's tried but they all say he's got to have experience before he can get a job. Catch twenty-two, that's called. Know what I mean?'

'Yeah. I guess . . . Oh . . . nearly forgot.'

'What?'

'You know.'

Chris leaned out as Jimmy hopped from his bed and put the light on again. 'Owww. You've blinded me! I can't see. I shall never play the violin again! My career's ruined. Anyway, Jimmy, what're you doing? Oh! Course.'

His young brother, wearing only a faded pair of pyjama bottoms, was pressing his back against the edge of the door, straining every sinew of his body.

'You're wasting your time,' teased Chris. 'You'll never even reach five feet.'

'I will,' Jimmy retorted, reaching with a stub of pencil in his right hand and touching the door with it.

'You're on your toes,' accused his older brother. 'I can see light under your heel.'

'Can't.'

'Can!'

'Can't!!!'

'Quiet. You'll have Mum an' Dad up. Well? What's the news?'

Jimmy peered at the mark, trying to decide whether there'd been any change. He checked with his father's old steel rule. 'Yeah! Four-feet-six-and-five-eighths.'

'Terrific,' applauded Chris, sarcastically. 'Now turn off the light and go back to bed.'

'All right,' said Jimmy.

3 While Chris was cleaning his teeth after breakfast, Jimmy surreptitiously measured himself once more against the bedroom door. To his irritation, the extra eighth of an inch had somehow disappeared overnight.

He stared moodily out of the window, across the scrubby garden, baked dusty brown by the summer's heat. Past the fences to the railway line. As he watched, one of Southern Region's morning commuter trains went snaking by. Its rumbling engines made the loose pane of glass rattle. Jimmy could see that the carriages were packed full with brimming rows of white faces, many hidden behind folded newspapers.

Kate had been in a bad mood at breakfast. She had picked at the delicious pancakes that their father had cooked for them, and only sipped at a beaker of black instant coffee. Dad had pressed her. Mum was still upstairs, getting herself ready to call in at a couple of local employment agencies to try and find some office temping during the school's summer holidays.

'Oh, it's the bloke who's assistant buyer on my floor.'

'Hill? Is that the guy's name?'

'That's him. Kenny the Menace, we all call him. Suffers from the disease of the desert, doesn't he?'

Dad's face had been puzzled. 'How's that, Kate. Run it by me again?' Despite his time in England, Burge Marvin had never lost his Americanisms.

'Disease of the desert! Wandering palms! You know. Fancies himself with girls.'

'Complain, Kate. Or I'll complain for you. Or your mother will.'

'What's the point, Dad? He's been there for donkeys . . . they'd never take the word of someone like me over dear Mr Hill. He's been married to one of the directors' daughters for years. No. There's no point in . . . but I tell you what. The next time he says a word out of place to me, with his nasty grin, then I'll clock him one right in his teeth. And he can take his job and he can . . .'

At that point she'd jumped up and run from the breakfast table, to her room, slamming her door. Dad and Jimmy, left alone, looked at each other over the muesli packet.

Jimmy wasn't that keen on summer holidays. The Marvin family hadn't been able to afford a real holiday for six years, though Mum and Dad generally tried to manage a trip out to the sea or into the country a couple of times each summer.

Without a bike, and low on pocket money, the lazy, hazy days dragged wearily by. Sometimes he'd go up the park and throw a football round with a few mates from the Victors. He'd tried to get a part-time job down the market, but everyone told him to go away and grow up a bit and then come back in ten years.

The best things were gridiron training and the big charity match to look forward to. But things hadn't always been that good at Elmstead Victors. Jimmy remembered his first two or three visits up there. With no gear of his own, except for a pair of soccer boots with half the studs gone and his cut-down jeans.

When he'd seen the Under Fourteen team's coach, Jerry Meredith, he'd very nearly turned on his heel and gone straight home. Jerry was a skinny American, stooped over, with a wrinkled face. He looked like a single puff of wind would blow him away. Jimmy's guess was that the coach was around eighty years old.

He found out a little later that he was only in his early sixties. And that he'd played for the Philadelphia Eagles for sixteen years as a cornerback. Mainly in the nineteen forties under their famous coach, Earle 'Greasy' Neale.

At his first sight of Jimmy, Jerry Meredith very nearly told the stocky little boy to turn on his heel and go on home. 'You're a tad on the not very tall side, son,' he'd said. 'And you can't really turn up here in gear like that and look to play for the Victors.'

Over the next couple of weeks Jerry Meredith was to bitterly regret both those statements.

Almost immediately others boys on his squad took him aside and laid out the difficult financial position of the Marvin family, explaining that what Jimmy had turned up in was, literally, the best he could manage.

And the dig about size soon proved an indigestible morsel for the elderly coach.

Jimmy's enthusiasm for the sport was instantly obvious. He was intensely keen and motivated to do well. Also, Meredith found the boy had an almost encyclopaedic fund of knowledge about American Football. Who played for who and what kind of record they had. Who'd beaten who and when and how.

To start with Jimmy was tried out at punt return. Fielding the long kicks deep into their own territory and trying to run the ball back as far as possible, it's one of the key specialist positions in the gridiron game.

The Victors had a good reputation and were one of the most winningest teams south of the Thames. They'd been founded in 1984 and Coach Meredith had worked hard to produce a well-drilled, professional unit. Any new boy coming in was likely to be tested by the others. And tested hard.

Uncomfortable in a borrowed helmet, Jimmy had faced the first kick, butterflies busy in his stomach. His mouth was dry and the palms of his hands seemed to be coated with a mixture of sweat and slippery oil. He wiped them on his jeans and swallowed, taking deep breaths like his father had told him. The ball hung in the air, turning end over end with an unnatural slowness. He was aware of the special kicking squad thundering downfield towards him.

He dropped it.

But he caught the second kick, making a half dozen yards before he was overwhelmed.

The third time he caught it and made nearly twenty yards, dodging around two of the rushing players.

The fourth kick was difficult, bouncing short, but Jimmy was still able to cover it safely.

The fifth was a high, spiralling punt, the wind catching the ball, making it slant away from him. With a desperate lunge, the boy reached it, holding onto it by his finger-tips. He heard the voice of the coach, praising the catch. But Jimmy Marvin wasn't finished yet.

Glancing up he saw that the charging boys had slowed, expecting him to drop the punt. He set off, digging in, sprinting around the first two players, brushing aside a half-hearted tackle from a third. His own team saw there was a chance for him and started throwing in some ferocious blocks to open a path for him. Suddenly he was in the clear, with only the kicker to beat. The boy hurled himself desperately at Jimmy, managing to tip his ankle. It threw him off balance, but he kept going, recovering, finally running the ball the entire way back into the end-zone for a superb touchdown.

It was a great moment. Something bright to treasure in a world that was often low on triumphs.

Coach Meredith put the small boy straight into the team for the next match, giving him some extra time and counselling at their training sessions.

After three games Jimmy Marvin had scored two touchdowns and had a punt-return average of well over thirty yards per carry. What really impressed the elderly American was the unswerving dedication and fire of the boy. He was certainly one of the smallest players in the league, but he was delighted to have the opportunity to run at lads a foot taller and four stone heavier than himself.

'You like hitting, Jimmy?' said Meredith, after the boy had been with him for a month.

'Yeah. It's a good feeling to go hard and fair at someone and rattle them.'

'And you don't mind being hit?'

'Not so long as it's fair. Don't like anyone who tries to play foul.'

'Sure thing. You see, Jimmy, the world's full of ball-players who like the glamour. The run and the charge. Not that many relish being put down hard and often. I figure you could be one that does.'

The boy shrugged. 'Don't mind. I can take it. Just wish you'd . . .'

'What?'

'Sounds flash, Coach. Only been with the squad and I don't sort of . . .'

'You weren't going to say you'd like to try out as a running back, were you, Jimmy?' Jerry Meredith's eyes twinkled.

The boy's jaw dropped. 'How did? I never told nobody at all. Apart from my brother. Oh! Was it Chris grassed on me, Coach? I'll do him if it was him. That's rotten.'

The American laughed delightedly. 'Course he didn't. I was going to give you a go at it. Despite being real short . . . I mean, stocky, despite that, you go hard as any kid in the league. You could be a natural at running back, Jimmy. Give it a go.'

Coach Meredith was right. Jimmy Marvin was a natural at the position. Taking the ball direct from the hands of their quarterback, and then going hard for the end-zone.

By July he'd established himself as one of the most feared runners in any team. Close to the line he was almost unstoppable. Defences double-teamed him, and he still managed to score. One of the coach's favourite sayings about offences was that they had to get to the end-zone. 'Through, round or over,' he'd say. 'It don't signify how you do it.'

Jimmy did them all. But the one that gave him the greatest delight was 'over'. Standing back about eight steps when the team had a down within a couple of yards of the goal-line. The ball would be snapped to the quarterback and Jimmy was already moving. Powering in with short strides, clutching the ball and leaping high into the air, clear over the grappling defenders, he'd plough through to the end-zone.

Jimmy was always hungry for more work. He still played punt return and was even in the special team for kick offs and punt coverage. His fierce tackling became an instant legend throughout the American Football youth teams in the area. For a player to spot the diminutive figure in the Victors' colours of maroon and navy blue was often enough to cause a fumble before he'd even been tackled.

It's always been a tradition in the gridiron game

that outstanding players get given nicknames. After Jimmy had run in a match-winning touchdown from the thirty-five, with only a minute remaining, giving the Elmstead team a victory over their old rivals from Blackheath, Coach Meredith decided it was time for the young running back to get christened.

'Watchin' you come through that big defence, I saw a kind of a vision of an acorn sprouting among the oaks,' he said. 'Guess from now on I'm calling you the Mighty Acorn, son.'

Jimmy would have preferred the 'Pocket Thunderbolt', but it was better than nothing.

The charity match against the Downham Destroyers was the biggest of the season. In another three weeks the Victors' Under Fourteens would be playing in their league final, and that would be the end of the season for them. Chris's team had done badly in the first half of the summer and wasn't going to make the Under Seventeen play-offs.

Mum and Dad were both coming to support their sons, and Kate had promised to try and get along for the third and fourth quarters. She was on her summer fortnight and was spending her time trying to find another job after the harassment at the store had become much worse. Her boyfriend, Roger, had already threatened to go and sort out Mr Hill, but had been persuaded instead to go with Kate for an interview in Oxford Street.

Chris and Jimmy had been up early, throwing a ball to each other down the middle of the road and trying to avoid the morning motorists. Chris fancied his chances against a younger team, even though Jim kept reminding him that the Destroyers would also be bringing down half a dozen older boys: 'And they got this Dave Sheppard quarterbacking and this other kid, Will Thomas, at wide receiver.'

'I'll flatten 'em both,' grinned Chris.

'That'll be the day,' said Jimmy. There'd been a John Wayne film on their failing black and white telly the previous night, and they'd all been trying out their impersonations of the great old western actor. Mum had been best at it.

'What time are we kicking off?' asked Dad. He'd been busy in the kitchen, making sandwiches for all of them and ladling out vacuum flasks of home-made soup.

'One o'clock,' replied Jimmy.

'Best start off around eleven-thirty,' suggested Mum. 'Give you time to get changed and ready and all. I'm nearly ready.'

Both his parents were in the kitchen when Jimmy eventually came down, bag packed with his gear. Dad had his arm around Mum's shoulder, pretending to nibble her throat like a vampire. She giggled helplessly, and pushed at him feebly to try and make him stop.

It was good to see them happy. Sometimes he thought how old they both looked. Sort of dragged down with tiredness. But he'd also noticed how they always tried to boost each other. If Dad had received another job rejection, but Mum came home from school having had a rotten time teaching Study Skills to Five F, then his father would put on a special meal and have the kettle singing when she came in.

'Postman's coming!' called Chris, out in the front garden.

'Won't have anything for us,' said Dad. 'Less'n it's a lot more bills.'

'Letter from Uncle Frank in Vermont,' shouted Jimmy's brother.

'Bung it on the table in the kitchen,' said Dad. 'The day my brother has something real important to tell us is the day that hell freezes over. Come on, you guys. Let's all go and play us some ball!'

Jimmy felt nervous.

Like he had at the first ever training session. He'd never seen such a big crowd. There was also a marching-band, an aerobatic display and a show of police dogs leaping over walls and chasing burglars, pulling them down by padded arms. A booming public address system introduced the teams and a squad of genuine officials from the adult League.

And there were the Downham Destroyers in their famous colours of silver and maroon.

Jerry had his whole squad around him. He was wearing his battered Eagles cap on the tight grey curls. 'I know you guys want to sneak a look at 'em. Go ahead. Look at 'em. See any of them with four legs or an extra pair of hands? Sure you don't. So they're human like us. Like most of us. They've got a good team, a great coach in Tom Nickleby, and one or two outstanding players. Chris Marvin.'

'Yeah, Coach?'

'Plenty of work from you today against Dave Sheppard and Wilburn Thomas.'

Jimmy looked across at the other team. Their coach was a skinny bearded man in glittering mirrored sunglasses. Standing with his two star players, stooped over them, talking intently.

33

Wilburn Thomas was their receiver; a tall, well-built black kid, wearing the number 83. Jimmy guessed that he must be a fan of the Dolphins' Mark Clayton, whose number that was. Sheppard was a solemn-looking boy, with a bright, intelligent face. He was carrying his helmet and wore the number 16. Jimmy's knowledge of the gridiron game told him that Dave must be a fan of the Forty-Niners' great quarterback, Joe Montana. He looked enviously at the smart turn-out of the other team. Some of their gear carried the names of local firms that must be sponsoring them, not like the more ragged appearance of his own team.

The Downham boys came over and started shaking hands with the Victors, talking about who played where and making joking threats to each other. Someone patted Jimmy on top of his head and he turned round, seeing Dave and Wilburn grinning at him.

'You the mascot, mate?' asked Dave. Smiling at his friend. 'Neat mascot. It's brill, isn't it, Will?'

'Yeah. A rave, Dave.'

Jimmy had to struggle to control his temper, though he knew the others were just trying to get a rise out of him. 'You just watch me, mate. If we get close to your end-zone, you'll see the mascot runnin' it in to score. Stop you grinning, won't it?'

The two Destroyers both grinned, slapping him on the back. 'Actually,' said Dave Sheppard, 'Coach Nickleby's been doing his homework on your lot. He reckons you're a bit good. And you got a big, big brother, don't you? We'll be watching out for you.'

34

Wilburn shook Jimmy's hand, checking out his number. 'Twenty-six? Mike Haddix of the Eagles?'

'No.'

Dave tried, while also shaking hands. 'Not that common a number. Jann McElroy, the Raiders' safety? No. Can't be if you're a running back. Matt Suhey from the Bears?'

'No,' said Jimmy, impressed at the knowledge of the two boys which certainly matched his own.

'Got it,' said Dave, triumphantly. 'Of course. And he's only five-foot-six. Little Train. Lionel James of the Chargers.'

'That's it. Anyway, hope it's a great game. Good luck, guys. See you after.'

He watched as Dave and Wilburn walked back to rejoin the group around their coach, thinking how much he'd liked them at a first meeting.

Chris came over and spoke to his younger brother. The kick-off was only a couple of minutes away.

'They seem all right, those Destroyers. Their quarterback came an' chatted a bit. Said I reminded him of some guy he'd played against over in the States.'

Jimmy was very impressed. 'They played football over there?'

'Yeah. San Francisco, he said. There's this big kid called Tommy something. Axler, I think it was. They said this kid was called the "Mean Machine".'

Jimmy could see that Chris was really flattered at that.

*

Once the game started and the Downham Destroyers' offense got the ball, all the flourishing friendships were immediately buried. Chris Marvin was on the field and got his first taste of the dynamic duo from north of the Thames, Sheppard and Thomas.

Wilburn picked the ball up on a simple timing pattern and ran straight back past the Elmstead cornerback, Tony Chapman. Only a despairing tackle from the free safety, Andy Franklin, bringing the flying teenager down on the five yard line, saved the score in the first thirty seconds.

First and goal to go, on the five. The supporters from Downham were cheering and waving scarves. The Elmstead fans were deathly silent.

The offence chose to go on the ground for the first down, moving towards where Chris Marvin was waiting. He shrugged off one block and barrelled into a tough Downham boy called Jack Crystal, jarring the ball loose from his grip. It bobbled agonisingly around until Chris himself managed to scramble over on his hands and knees and gain possession of it at their eight yard line.

That put Jimmy and the offence on the field. Not wanting to let their opponents settle, Coach Meredith called three successive pass plays. But every one was incomplete, one almost being picked up by Downham's Jamie Hunter.

This brought on the Elmstead punting team. Wilburn fell back deep to return the kick. Jimmy saw the black boy's eyes seeking him out, watching him, looking around to see where the gaps might be for his punt return.

Wilburn caught the kick, moving immediately into top gear, legs pounding, his speed starting to move him away from the Elmstead coverage. But Jimmy kept his cool, not committing himself too early to the faster runner. He timed his tackle perfectly, angling his body so that he caught the Downham 83 below the knees with his shoulder. Will Thomas was flipped clear into the air in a punishing somersault but just managed to hang on to the football.

'Good tackle, son!' called Jerry Meredith.

From the other side of the field came the bellowing voice of the Downham Coach, Tom Nickleby. 'Wrong, Jerry. Not a good tackle! A *great* tackle!'

Jimmy was up first and offered a hand to the other boy to help him. Wilburn was shaking his head. 'Wow! You give a big lick for someone your size, man,' he said.

'Hey! I'm four-feet-six-and-seven-eighths, you know.'

The other boy grinned. 'Yeah. That's just what I meant.'

Downham restarted well with a big first down pass to Mike Howell. But on their next play Chris bowled over his blocker and got to the quarterback, sacking Dave Sheppard for a net loss of six yards.

On second and sixteen the Downham offence went for one of their well-rehearsed trick plays. Dave took the snap and passed it off to Jack Crystal who came on a wide sweep, towards Chris Marvin. From the sideline Jimmy yelled to his brother to make the tackle.

Just as he moved in to make the hit, the big Destroyer flipped the ball in a lateral pass to Wilburn, sprinting a reverse in the opposite direction. The whole defence was completely wrong-footed. Committed to the tackle, Chris sent Crystal flying and the two boys hit the dry turf in a tangle of arms and legs.

Wilburn was round the end of the defensive line, feinting and side-stepping, his move throwing the cornerback, Tony Chapman. The powerful black receiver coasted the rest of the way into the end zone, spiking the ball on the grass. Running back with a broad smile, he leaped into a hand-slapping high five with his delighted quarterback.

Chris Marvin trudged dejectedly to the side of the field, where Coach Meredith patted him on the shoulder.

'You got beat by the best, son. Never no shame in that. We'll come back at 'em.'

The restart after the extra point didn't bring much immediate joy to the Elmstead Victors. A tough lineman called Mark McLeod sacked their quarterback Hebron Wayman, for a loss of eight yards on their first down.

Behind the line of scrimmage, flexing his fingers nervously, Jimmy Marvin waited for a chance. On second and eighteen, Jerry Meredith sent in the signal that would use Number 26.

'Red left swing,' was the call. 'Hut, hut, hut,' the ball snapped back into Hebron's fingers on the third count.

McLeod once again got good penetration, reaching for Jimmy almost as soon as the diminutive running back had his hands on the pass. With a duck and a weave Jim slipped under the tackle, spotting a hole in the defensive line. One of the imported sixteen-year-olds dived at him, but ended on the turf, fingers filled with nothing but grass.

A tall Downham linebacker, called Rufus Smith, also had a chance at Jimmy but the back exploded into him, sending him staggering backwards, caught off-balance by the unexpected aggression of the much smaller boy.

It was a last-ditch effort by a defender, Jamie Hunter, that finally shoved Jimmy out of bounds. But his great run had carried his team all the way down to the Destroyers' twenty-four yard line.

On the next play a sixteen yard pass from Hebron took the Victors within field goal range. They tried for the ten yards on their next three downs but the Downham defence held them at bay. Paul Allen came on and slotted home the field goal, taking the score to seven-three in favour of the Destroyers.

The rest of the first half was running out scoreless, with the defences dominating. It was obvious to both coaches that the inclusion of a few of the older boys, just for this one charity game, had actually unbalanced both their squads. Easy, familiar plays went down and there was a greater than usual number of fumbles, sacks and interceptions.

Tom Nickleby used Wilburn sparingly, trying to give some of the other boys in his squad a run-out. Also, having seen the way Jimmy Marvin had demolished his star receiver, he didn't want to risk him too much in what was only a friendly.

Just before the clock for the first half ticked out, Chris broke through and sacked Dave Sheppard again, forcing them to punt. There were only twenty-eight seconds remaining in the half.

Jimmy was lined deep, watching the ball, locked into total concentration. Not hearing the cheering of both sets of supporters, closing out the sound of his mother's voice, soaring above the rest, urging him to go for it. Coach Meredith had told him he'd already managed to notch up over sixty rushing yards. Against such a tough team, he was well pleased. He felt properly warmed up, ready for one last charge to end the half.

He caught the ball cleanly on his own fifteen yard line. Beginning to angle towards the left, he saw that he had no blockers on that side and the whole of the Downham special team seemed to be bearing down on him. Without changing pace, he switched direction, slipping the first tackle with a hand-off.

Suddenly, Chris was ahead of him, clearing away a path like a bulldozer through a sheet of wet cardboard. One last devastating block, Jimmy hurdling the jumble of arms and legs, throwing his head back and sprinting flat out. It was then the roar of the spectators got to him, lifting him on. The kicker, as so often, was the last line of the defence. As so often, his attempted tackle was pathetically feeble and Jimmy was gone.

Clear into the end-zone for a marvellous touchdown. He jumped in the air and got ready to spike the ball, but changed his mind at the last moment and handed it to the official who'd signalled his score.

Chris was the first there to congratulate him and the two brothers gleefully exchanged the sliding handshake know as 'giving some skin'.

The point after was good and the teams went to their half-time break with the Elmstead Victors leading ten points to seven over the favourites from north of the river.

Tom Nickleby nodded his appreciation at Jimmy. 'Any time you want a free transfer, son,' he said. 'Any time at all.'

'Don't relax. Don't give up. Don't get careless. They'll come back at you. It's not won yet, guys. Not by a country mile, it's not.'

Jerry Meredith was a good judge of a game.

On their first possession in the third quarter, Elmstead were under pressure and had to punt. While Jimmy watched open-mouthed, Wilburn Thomas caught the poor kick and simply outran everyone into the end-zone without a finger being laid on him. Jim'd never seen anyone able to switch the burners on like that and it made him realise that he was looking at some genuine class. Jimmy also felt that the great score had somehow diminished his own achievements.

Despite that feeling, he still managed to total up another one-hundred-and-nine yards rushing for himself. But Elmstead managed only one more score in the last two quarters of the game. Wide receiver, Andy Hopper, caught a bullet pass from Hebron from inside the Downham ten and dived in untouched.

Coach Nickleby pulled Wilburn from the game after his electrifying touchdown and Dave Sheppard was also pulled at the end of the third quarter, giving the reserve quarterback of the Destroyers, Steve Bond, a chance. But on his very last play Dave showed his class with a perfectly weighted pass to big Jack Crystal, enabling him to pick up another touchdown for the visitors.

In the last few minutes of the final quarter, despite great pass-rush pressure from Chris Marvin and the defence, Steve Bond moved his team steadily down the field. Ending up in field goal range and a final score of twenty-four to seventeen.

Jimmy felt utterly drained by the game. The tension beforehand and the pace that it had been played at had knocked him out, and seeing players of the skill of Dave and Wilburn had given him a lot to think about.

Coach Nickleby had come to him and Chris while they were saying their goodbyes to the Downham team and patted them both on the back.

'Very well played, both of you. I could fit either of you into our starting line-up if you ever moved house.

Don't suppose you move house very often though, do you?'

'You'd be surprised,' said Jimmy.

The family walked home together through the late afternoon sunshine. Mum and Dad insisted on still holding each other's hand, to the embarrassment of the three children. Kate and Roger were in front, locked in a hissing argument about jobs. Chris and Jimmy brought up the rear, talking about the game and remembering certain plays. Mainly ones where they'd managed to distinguish themselves.

'I got some cheap cuts of white fish on the market,' said Burgess Marvin as they turned in the gate. 'I'll do it *en croute*.'

'On what?' said Chris.

Burge laughed teasing his tall son: '*Croute*, you shambling retard, Christopher! How I come to be your father is something that constantly keeps me awake during the long winter nights. Why you? Why couldn't I have adopted some nice, gentle, intelligent child?' He sighed, melodramatically. '*Croute* means cooked in a light, fluffy pastry shell, Chris. I shall serve it with some piped duchesse potatoes, fresh peas, and plain white sauce. And I've done a special strawberry flan for dessert. They were cheap at that little shop down the High Road.'

Mum sighed, licking her lips. 'I don't know how you do it, Burge. Not on what we bring in. I sometimes wonder what you could do with food if you had

43

a real budget and could buy and cook what you wanted?'

'I reckon we'd all burst,' said Jimmy.

'I could of eaten one more helping, Mum,' Jimmy said, plaintively.

'It's could *have* as you well know. Just go and get on with the washing-up. It's your turn.'

As he was collecting the dishes, the boy noticed the airmail letter still unopened on the table. 'Don't forget this, Dad,' he said.

His father took it, slitting the envelope open with his nail. 'It won't be important. Brother Frank never has anything that important to tell us. Let's see now . . .'

5

'Read it again, Chris.'

'Play it again, Sam.'

'What?'

'It's a line from one of those crummy old gangster movies that Mum and Dad keep watching on telly dead late at night. You know. Someone says: "Play it again, Sam".'

Jimmy leaned out of his bunk. 'Look. Just read the rotten letter, will you? Or give it here, and I'll read it again.'

His brother handed down the pale blue letter, crumpled from being devoured a couple of dozen times by all the family. Its effect was so startling that it had even postponed Dad's promised cod *en croute* for nearly two hours.

The familiar clipped black handwriting was edged with an occasional tiny sketch in the margins. Just holding it brought back memories to Jimmy of the couple of times that his uncle had visited England. Once had been when Chris had been adopted.

The families were interwoven.

Jimmy and Kate's mother, Beth, had visited America some twenty years ago to be a bridesmaid for her best friend from school and college, Laura. She'd been marrying Francis Marvin. There she'd met his

45

younger brother, Burgess, and they'd fallen in love, marrying only three weeks after they'd first met. This had always seemed a bit sloppy to Jimmy and Kate. Beth's sister, Janine, had been married a year later, to an English friend of Burgess Marvin. All three couples had enjoyed a lot of happiness until the dark shadow settled on Janine and her husband.

Driving home from the cinema on a foggy, cold November evening, a jack-knifing artic' had wiped them both away. After interminable family conferences, it was agreed that the best thing would be for Chris, then just ten and an only child, to be adopted. So Burge and Beth Marvin acquired another son.

Uncle Frank lived with Aunt Laura in a white house in a village called North Strafford, in the northeastern state of Vermont. They had two children – Eddy who was fourteen and Angelina who was sixteen. Frank Marvin owned a successful gift shop, with some good quality antiques, next door to a run-down fast food café in his home village.

The letter began in typical Uncle Frank manner. Jimmy remembered him best for his booming voice and ceaseless good humour.

'Hi, Brits. How tall, Jimmy? Up to six-feet-tall yet? Guess not. Last report was four-feet-four-and-a-quarter.'

Jimmy couldn't remember how long ago that must have been. Not too long. The mark on the door had been edging upwards with a gratifying speed over the last few weeks.

'Can't waste time on social chit-chat, guys. Something is happening, and I *do* know what it is, Mr Jones.'

'What did Dad say that bit meant, Chris? This Mr Jones bloke?'

'It's a line from one of them old Bob Dylan songs Dad and Uncle Frank are always goin' on about.'

'Oh, yeah. I remember.' He carried on reading the letter.

'You remember the guy next door? The man who gave cooking a bad name? Cold soup and melted ice-cream. Beef-burgers with bits of horse-shoe still in 'em? More grease than the Acropolis!'

'He means "Greece", not "grease", doesn't he?' said Jimmy. Chris didn't answer him.

'Well, he's finally run the business into the ground. Trade went down the tube and he's selling up. He's asking a crazy price. Unless he finds some loony-tune, New York yuppie to buy it as a tax loss he'll never get it. But, brother, I can buy him out at a sensible price. You know what you and I have joked about all these years? Well, it's not a joke any more, Burge.'

'Go for it, Dad,' said Jimmy, under his breath. But Chris heard him.

'You got to the good bit, yet?'

'Yeah. Want me to read it out to you?'

'Go on.'

'"Burge, The Olde Roaste Beefe can move out of the pages of legend and into the pages of history! We can do it. I got the bread and now I can get the place for it. Right smack next door. You know the class of

47

clientele that dig what we sell. They'd dig some genuine class English cooking at the same time. In the summer and fall this is heavy tourist country. Think about it. But only for ten seconds. Call me collect and tell me when you're all coming over. There's plenty for Beth to do and lotsa work locally for Kate. And the boys can play football for real."'

'Again,' urged Chris.

'We can play football for real. It's not that far to go and watch the Patriots. And the Lakers against the Celtics at basketball.'

'And the Boston Red Sox at Fenway Park. Watching baseball from the bleachers. Oh, Jim . . . it'd be great, wouldn't it?'

Jimmy Marvin found it difficult to slip into sleep that night, his whole body brimmed with excitement.

Excitement, mixed with a sizeable dose of apprehension.

'Family conference,' Burge Marvin announced to his three children the next morning as they all sat at the breakfast table.

'We going, Dad?' asked Kate, through a mouthful of wholewheat toast, dripping with lime-flower honey.

He shook a finger at her. 'No way, daughter. Not the way the Marvin family make their decisions. It hasn't been that way since you lot were old enough to understand our problems. Mum and I have always tried to involve you lot in what's going on with us. For better or worse, like the preacher says.'

'Pass the peanut butter, Chris,' said Jimmy. Somehow he didn't want to get involved in such an important discussion. In case the suggestion was thrown out.

'Looks like being a nice day,' said Mum. 'Weather forecast's good. Probably means we'll have hurricanes if Mr Fish has anything to do with it.'

'Where're we going, Mum?' asked Chris, helping himself to a chunky helping of the peanut butter before he passed it on to Jimmy. The way of big brothers throughout history.

'Thought we might go down to Saint Mary Cray on the train and just walk out into the country. Dad'll do a picnic. There's that little river we've been to before. You know where I mean?'

'Yeah. That'd be cool. And then we can talk about the . . . about the letter from Uncle Frank?'

Mum nodded. 'We can. Obviously Dad and I have given it a lot of thought. Don't reckon we got to sleep until the dawn chorus, did we, love?'

'No,' agreed Dad. 'But there's lots of things to think about. Affecting all of us. We want you three to think long an' hard about it. Try and think of the good *and* the bad. Talk it over amongst yourselves if'n you want to do that. We'll leave about noon.'

'High noon,' said Jimmy.

The atmosphere on the train south was oddly tense and strained. The taboo subject was the one that was preoccupying all of them.

Dad centred his thoughts on how he'd cope with

going back to his homeland. A crippled failure, going to depend on the help of his older brother.

Mum was worried about whether she'd find work over in Vermont and how the boys' schooling would be affected. And how Kate would manage a break-up with Roger. And how her own mother would survive with them all gone.

Roger had once said that he couldn't live without Kate, but the girl thought that he was just saying that because he guessed it sounded all romantic. A new life in a new world. She'd seen pictures of Vermont, of the brilliant hues of autumn and then massive falls of clean snow, piled fifteen feet high along the side of the rural roads. But, would she really be able to get a job there, away from the persistent attention of Mr Hill?

Chris was worrying about all his mates, and whether he'd be able to make new friends if they moved.

Jimmy looked out of the window, not seeing the smudge of suburban houses as they blurred by him. Patterns of washing danced on clothes-lines and toddlers rode toy horses. Cars were cleaned and lawns mowed. On a hillside a few kites strained against the summer breeze, crimson and gold under the blue sky. South London went about its business and they were going to talk about leaving it all behind them. Them. The Marvin family!

The totality of it almost overwhelmed the thirteen-year-old boy.

'Right,' said Dad.

The picnic was over. Only Chris had managed to

eat anything like his usual amount. Kate had only picked at a fresh shrimp salad in a freezer box. Jimmy had forced down a couple of whipped egg-and-cress sandwiches. Neither Mum nor Dad had tackled the spread with anything like their usual enthusiasm for food. But they'd finished the bottle of white wine that Dad had splashed out on. The three children had drained the litre of apple juice.

It was scorchingly hot.

While the picnic was being laid out ready, Jimmy and Chris had walked into the sloping meadow, away from the shrunken stream, and tossed a football to each other. Butterflies skittered low over the dry grass, and swallows and martins circled skittishly, snapping up the myriad tiny insects.

Now they were all resting around the curling sandwiches and the stained paper plates. Dad had wrapped up the uneaten banana loaf and put it back in the plastic box, warning them that it would have to be eaten up for supper.

Kate was on her back, knees drawn up, staring at the sky. Chris was on his stomach, chin on his hands, gazing past his parents towards the beech coppice at the head of the field. Jimmy was cross-legged, listening to the singing of the brook over the moss-stained rocks.

Mum and Dad sat together, like a pair of bookends. Her hand rested gently on his arm. Their shoulders just touched.

'Right,' said Dad, once more. 'Who wants to start? Kate?'

'No, thanks. I reckon you an' Mum should go first. Tell us what you reckon.'

'Yeah,' said Chris. 'If you don't want to go, then there's not a lot of point in us saying we like the idea, is there?'

Jimmy said nothing.

Beth Marvin nodded approvingly. 'I think that's right, don't you, Burge?'

'Sure.'

She hesitated. 'I think that this is about the biggest decision we've ever faced as a family. Maybe the biggest that we'll ever have to confront.'

Dad took over. 'When I screwed up my back, it didn't seem too bad at first. Then it just got worse. No job. Money gettin' smaller and bills gettin' bigger. Fact is . . . the future isn't that bright. Rent's way behind again and they're talking 'bout finally puttin' us on a section of an estate, further in. That's where all the . . . all the no-hopers finish up. Short step from there to hostels and bein' split up.'

Nobody spoke. None of the children had realised just how bleak the future had become. Over the brow of the hill they heard the snarling of a motor-bike, sending a flock of pigeons fluttering from the trees nearby.

'I'm not saying that this chance could be the last chance. I guess . . . No. I think the truth might be, folks, that this *could* be our last chance to break out of the chains. But that doesn't mean it'll be easy. Not if I know my brother, Francis. And there's a whole slew of problems to sort out. Jobs. School. Visas. You've all got dual nationality, so that should be all right. And then there's personal considerations,' looking at his daughter.

'What 'bout Gran?' asked Jimmy.

'Nice of you to think of her, love,' said Mum. 'I've already spoken to her, this morning. I popped over for a chat. Said it was a possibility and asked how would she feel?'

'What did she say?' asked Chris.

'She said we could have her National Savings money if it might help us make it over there.'

Dad broke the fresh silence. 'So, it's up to you three now. Let's hear what you think. Everything.'

Kate looked at Chris, then both of them looked at Jimmy. For thirty or so beats of the heart none of them said anything. Finally, it was Jimmy who spoke for them all.

'Why not?' he said.

Life became like a dream.

Sometimes speeded up. Rushing to meetings with teachers and getting forms signed. Standing in line by the often vandalised phone box on a windswept corner, a quarter mile away, waiting for a few snatched words with relations in Vermont.

Sometimes it slowed down, like running through treacle. Every step painful and laborious. Days plodded by when nothing seemed to happen at all.

Yet, despite all this, progress was made.

The weather changed for the worse, the sweltering heat and bright gold days vanishing behind the skirts of a chill easterly wind. Rain slanted across the terraced rows of South London houses, driving children indoors. The local playing-field became a wintery quagmire and the last regular game of the season for the Elmstead squad boys was washed out.

Chris's season finished on that miserable anti-climax and he moped around home like a tiger with the toothache.

Jimmy's season had just one match left. The League final against their old rivals, the Bromley Bears. A team they'd already beaten once by a last-minute field-goal earlier in the summer. But now the Victors had

54

player problems. Several of their starting squad were going to be away on unavoidable family holidays and they'd be using some of their reserves.

One thing that caused a lot of joking at their last training session was a piece of news from Coach Jerry Meredith.

'Gonna make you stars,' he grinned. 'Bunch of students have got some kind of summer project. They're videoing Hither Green during the vacation – the people at work and at play. And you guys get to be some of their players. They'll vid' the final against the Bears.'

Immediately everyone started posing, flicking back hair and testing chins for the first signs of any designer stubble. Jimmy was nearest the scratched steel mirror in their training-room and he automatically glanced at himself, checking the reflec.

The coach clapped his hands together to silence the chatter and laughter. 'Worry about lookin' good on the field, team! You know that this is the big one for this year. Next year there'll be changes. We all know 'bout Jimmy Marvin, our own Mighty Acorn, who's goin' away to try life in the land of the free and the home of the brave. We gotta win this for Jimmy.'

There were two good omens on the morning of the match.

The postman brought a massive envelope that contained all of their documents, tickets, visas and brochures for their emigration. That was a word that

Jimmy hadn't heard before. 'Emigration'. It sounded very formal.

And very final.

The other good thing was when Jimmy took his careful pre-breakfast measure against the edge of the bedroom door.

Over the last month, the fractions had been piling steadily up. Even Dad grudgingly admitted that Jim was going through a 'growing-burst'.

'Four-feet-eight inches,' Jimmy whooped, checking it one more time to be certain. Somehow it seemed a lot taller than four-feet-seven-and-seven-eighths. 'Hear that, Chris?'

His older brother, still dozing with his head buried under the blankets, clapped his hands together once. 'One clap, Jimmy. That's all you get. One clap! Now shut up. I need my beauty sleep.'

'Nobody needs it more than you,' sniggered Jimmy, dodging out of the room just in time to avoid the hurled pillow.

The days of leaden skies and weeping rain finally ended during the late morning of game-day. Streaks of pallid blue appeared from the west, and a watery sun broke through.

Kate had promised to come along and watch with Chris and both parents. She'd handed in her notice, delighting in finally having the opportunity to tell the obnoxious Mr Hill what she really thought of him. On the other side of the coin, she was having terrible problems trying to persuade Roger that she had to go to the States with the rest of the family.

Departure day was set. The last Friday in August. Now less than a fortnight away.

As the two teams lined up for the kick-off, Jimmy thought he'd never felt as nervous as this. There'd never been a game in his life so far that he more wanted to win.

The whistle blew and they were off.

It was a little after nine that evening when Jimmy pressed the brass bell-push set in the centre of his Gran's front door. He'd walked through the quiet streets, parallel to the railway line, arriving close by Hither Green Station. He'd told his parents that he wanted to go for a stroll on his own to try and unwind after the tension of the afternoon's big game.

In the stillness he could hear his grandmother shuffling down the passage from her back parlour in her down-at-heel slippers. Peering through the stained glass of the door panels he could just make out her stooped figure. There was the familiar rattling of chains, sliding of bolts, and clicking of security locks.

'Hello, Jim. You're a bit of a stranger. Come on in, love.'

He caught the scent of the peppermints she always sucked and he could hear the blaring of the telly she'd been watching. It was of one of her favourite game shows, with the sound turned up loud. Gran had been going a bit deaf lately.

'Want a cuppa, Jimmy? Or I got a bottle of fizzy lemonade, though it's probably a bit flat by now. I bought it last Christmas, I think.' She gave her cackling laugh. When nobody was around she never bothered with her false teeth, and the lack of them made her cheeks sort of fold in and she seemed older. She was wearing a flowered dress with a navy blue cardigan, its pockets bulging with sweet wrappers.

'I'd like a cuppa, please, Gran,' he said. 'Shall I turn the telly off?'

'Course you can. Load of old rubbish. Don't know why I bother watchin' it.'

The boy sat down in a comfortably sagging armchair and glanced round the room. Wondering how many times he'd sat there. Wondering whether he'd ever sit there again.

Jim was always conscious of the contrast between Gran's home and the various houses that he'd lived in. She'd been born in the small terraced house in Leahurst Road. Her mother and father, Jimmy's great-grandparents, had moved there just after their own marriage. It had been Great-Grandfather Cedric who'd installed electricity in the house. He'd done it himself, and you could only turn off the landing light from the hall downstairs, which wasn't very convenient if you were going up to bed.

Gran's house was cluttered with furniture and ornaments, collected over sixty or seventy years. Every available bit of space had its own little pot or brass momento or glass, whereas their house never had any more than the barest of basics. Jimmy thought that

58

there was hardly anything in their home that he recalled from any previous homes. When they had to move, they could usually fit everything into a small van.

There was the whistling of the kettle and then the chinking of spoons in cups.

'Want a hand, Gran?'

'No thanks, ducks. The Good Lord gave me two hands of me own and that's all I need. Here you are, dear. Want a choccy digestive, Jim? Got some left over from me birthday.'

Since that had been in February, Jimmy decided to pass on the offer.

With a sigh, the old woman lowered herself into her own chair, which sagged even more alarmingly than the one that Jim was sitting in.

'Now, dear. To what do I owe this honour?'

'What?'

She cackled again. 'Didn't you know your Gran could speak posh if she wanted? I was askin' you why you'd come round?'

'Well, I was sort of out for a walk like and so I came round here.'

'What a load of horse manure!'

'Gran!'

'Don't come that with me, young Jimmy. You wasn't just passin' or anything like it. Did Beth put you up to this? Did she? Your Mum?'

'No.'

'Well . . .? I'm waitin' for the truth. Tell the truth and . . .'

'And shame the devil,' he completed. 'Yeah, I know that, Gran.'

'So. What's all this about? Wouldn't have somethin' to do with you goin' off across the sea, would it? That's my guess.'

'Yeah. It's to do with that.'

'And your mother didn't have nothin' to do with your comin' round?'

'No. She doesn't know.'

'Oh, secret, is it. Sure you don't want a biscuit or nothin' to eat?'

'No, thanks. It's just that I've been thinking about all of us going to America. I think that . . . Well, we all talked 'bout it a lot. We all reckon it's like a big chance.'

'Course it is, dear.'

'But, what about you, Gran?'

'What about me?'

'Yeah. Who's goin' to look after you when we've gone?'

'Well, that's real nice of you to worry about me, Jimmy, and that's the truth of it. Truth is, son, once your grandad had gone . . . and then Janine in that dreadful accident, I nearly give up then. Precious near went in the kitchen and stuck me head in the oven. But I didn't. And I'm glad. I've 'ad some good times on me own. Not the same, of course, but better than nothing.'

'You can come and see us.'

She burst into one of her cackling laughs, ending

up in a choking fit. Jimmy patted her on the back until she'd recovered her breath.

'Catch me up in one them planes! God didn't see fit to give me any wings, which means he don't want me flyin' around. No, I'm kidding you, son. Course I'll come over. But I manage most of the time on me own. Got a few friends can pop in for a chin-wag, and decent shops around here. Train to London if I need it. No, you gotta go, ducks.'

'But . . .'

Gran leaned forward and squeezed his hand. 'One day you'll get to be old, Jimmy, and you'll understand. I'm comin' to the last few miles of a long journey, son. And you're just setting off on the first steps. Wouldn't be right if I went and 'ung on your coat-tails, now would it? Course not. Now, you drink up your tea and then get along home with you.'

'Gran. Don't tell Mum . . .'

'Course not, dear. Our secret. And I do appreciate the thought, boy. I truly do. Now come 'ere and give your old Gran a hug, 'fore you go.'

Jimmy embraced her, feeling to his surprise how thin and frail she seemed to have become. It was like holding a sparrow in his hands. He kissed her on her dry, powdered cheek.

As he crossed over the road on his way home, Jimmy glanced behind him and saw the old lady silhouetted against the golden glow of her hall light. She waved a hand, leaning on the door-frame. He waved back. Watching as she closed the door, the rectangle of yellow light disappearing, leaving only blackness.

7

The viewing cinema at the local college was packed with boys. A scattering of parents were also there, with a few of the students who'd made the film of the game the previous weekend. Between the Elmstead Victors and the Bromley Bears for the championship of their American Football League.

Jimmy was sitting near the end of the front row of tip-up plastic seats. Partly looking forward to seeing the video and partly embarrassed at the idea of watching himself up there on the glittering white screen.

Chris had come along to see it, sitting in the row behind with a couple of his mates. Their father had hoped to get along but he'd had to go to a meeting with the local council about the details of handing over their house, less than ten days away, now.

Coach Jerry Meredith was down the front, talking to a bearded lecturer. Finally, glancing at his watch, the grizzled American clapped his hands together for silence.

'Right, you guys. Quieten down! Time to watch some football being played. Sorry we don't have Big John Madden to do the commentary. Mr Rosen here says they plan to do some more editing to it and add a musical track, but he thought that we'd like to see the rough cut before any of our starring roles end up on the cutting-room floor.'

'That's right, Mr Meredith. Sorry. Should call you "Coach", I believe. The current film lasts about thirty minutes. As you all know, we plan to edit it down as a part of the whole video about the area, so this is your one chance to see it in full.' The lecturer glanced to the rear of the hall. 'Lights please. Here we go.'

There was a mixture of applause and jeering as the first shot showed a very blurred view of the opening kick-off. But the focus quickly cleared. The camera had been set up behind the Bromley end-zone, waiting for their special team to face the kick.

Jimmy peered at the screen trying to locate himself in the picture, knowing that he'd be one of the Elmstead team in their maroon and blue. Poised to chase the kick down the field. Towards the camera.

'I'm not . . .' he began to say to himself, swallowing the words. But it was a surprise, and a disappointment, to realise how small he looked compared to some of the other boys on the squad. He seemed really tiny on the screen.

The cameraman had zoomed in on the ball, perched on its plastic tee, pulling back as the kick was made. He followed the spiralling torpedo as it soared high over the waiting return team.

'Nice one, Paul!' shouted someone in the viewing room.

Jimmy was perched on the edge of his seat, tense with excitement. He remembered this first play and couldn't wait to see it unwind.

The ball floated gently down, straight into the waiting arms of the Bromley player. But the second that he caught it, a small angry whirlwind shot on to the screen, like a shell fired from a mortar. Everyone roared as the Elmstead 26 exploded into the Bears' kick return boy, knocking him off his feet, caking mud between the bars of his helmet.

'Great one, Jim!' yelled Tony Chapman.

Chris smacked him on the shoulders approvingly. Coach Meredith leaned forwards and gave Jim the thumbs-up sign.

The diminutive cannonball stood over his obliterated victim, the camera lens zooming in on him. Jimmy suddenly recalled the moment and his face began to flush a deep crimson. He was enormously thankful that the screening room was in darkness because he saw himself, filling the picture. Spotting the camera on him he had jumped up and punched the air, waving a triumphant, menacing finger straight into the lens.

In his orange plastic seat, Jimmy shrank down, covering his face with his hands. Wishing that the earth could slide open on neat special effect rollers and swallow him up.

He heard Chris's voice, rising above the general laughter. 'See that? My little brother thinks he's L.T. from the Giants! That's really rich, Jimmy! What a killer!'

Jerry Meredith had to shout and ask them to stop the video for a moment to allow the boys time to recover themselves. Unfortunately, the freeze-frame was of Jimmy's face, eyes wide with the thrill of the moment, mouth half-open in a position that made him look like some kind of nutter.

This brought a second wave of merriment. Jerry Meredith's dry voice rose above the hubbub. 'Excellent tackle, Jimmy Marvin. Shame about afterwards.'

When the video resumed running, the laughter faded very quickly.

The Bromley Bears' quarterback, a skinny black teenager, took the snap at the very next play. The Victors' defence was showing blitz, but they never got the penetration they needed. One sideways jink and a lot of acceleration and the boy was away, evading some lazy, careless tackling to run the length of the pitch for an eighty-eight yard touchdown.

At least Elmstead succeeded in blocking the kick for the point after. Leaving the score at six points to nil at the end of the first quarter.

The door at the rear of the hall swung open and then crashed shut again. Everyone turned round to see Tony Chapman creeping in.

'Where've you been?' shouted Jimmy, glad to see someone else looking embarrassed. 'You was here a minute ago.'

'Had to go to the bog, didn't I? Door slipped out of me fingers when I come in again. Have I missed much?'

'Only the rottenest sequence of missed tackles in

the history of American Football,' said their Coach, drily.

The video film was running on. Chris Marvin pointed at the screen. 'There you are, Tony, my man. Just finished your pee in time.'

'Doesn't a pee in time save nine?' shrieked someone, overwhelmed by their own sense of humour.

'Simmer down. Watch and learn, guys. That's what you're here for,' said Jerry Meredith. This time allowing some genuine anger to creep into his voice, hushing the hall immediately.

The sleek cornerback had found himself a seat just along from Jimmy. Seeing himself on the screen he whispered: 'Thought I might miss meself, I remember this kick-off.'

Bromley Bears were lined up after their score and the missed extra point. The sound track surged and crackled with the roaring of their supporters and the squealing chants of their pretty group of teenage cheerleaders.

'I thought you *wanted* to miss it,' someone hissed from two rows behind.

'Yeah,' sighed Tony.

The ball was badly kicked, hardly rising more than fifteen feet from the glistening turf, rolling awkwardly, end over end.

Tony watched, silently like the others in the squad, seeing himself reach for the ball. Picking it out of the air but never quite managing to get a handle on it.

'Oh, no,' he said, quietly. 'I somehow hoped I might have caught it clean on the video. Instant replay of success.' He turned his head away, unable to watch the sequence.

The students who'd shot the film had chosen this part to stretch into some arty slow-motion, and had zoomed in on the boy's agonised expression as the damp ball skidded away from him, bobbling to the grass. Tony had then turned away on the screen as he lost control.

The Bromley fans cheered as a sea of boys fell on the ball. Most of them were the Bears.

Tony's error didn't seem to be too disastrous at the time. The Elmstead defence were fired up and held their opponents on the next three downs. But the long thirty-six yard field goal just clawed its way over the crossbar by its finger-nails, giving Bromley a lead of nine to nothing.

And that was the way it stayed through to the end of the second quarter.

The camera came with the dejected Elmstead team, eavesdropping on Coach Meredith's half-time talk to the squad. 'Turnovers kill ya, guys,' he said, surrounded by the weary, mudstained boys. 'There's a lot of you new to the plays, but that just means you gotta concentrate even more than usual. Listen to Hebron. Listen to his calls and try to remember what they mean. Second half I'll keep it as simple as I can. No trick plays. Nothing flash. Run it hard. And try not to fumble it when you get hit.'

That was about all he said. There was no inspirational speech to go out and win for their families and country. It wasn't that kind of a day.

Almost immediately the third quarter started the Elmstead supporters had something to cheer.

Watching it on the screen, Jimmy's previous blushes disappeared in pride. Bromley punted deep and he managed to make the difficult catch just inside his own end-zone.

'Go, bro!' yelled Chris Marvin from the seats just behind him.

The whole field stretched ahead of Jimmy, with every single player between him and the possibility of a score. With the first three attempted tackles he made no effort to avoid them or jink around them. Ball clutched tightly under his right arm he simply ran straight over them, leaving them sprawled on the grass. The camera followed him from the side of the pitch, the focus tight on him. Bodies appeared briefly on the edge of the screen and then seemed to vanish, bounced off by the sheer raw power of his run.

Jimmy watched the hash-marks on the field dance by under his running feet, counting himself up the field by the ten-yard lines.

'Half-way. Their forty . . . thirty . . . nearly got me there,' as he stumbled free of a despairing tackle. 'To the twenty, the ten . . . Goodbye!'

'Touchdown!' shouted everyone in the viewing-room, their voices almost drowned by the cheering and whooping that came crackling from the video speakers.

In the sudden stillness that followed, the only voice was Jerry Meredith. 'One-hundred-and-five yards, all the way' he said, almost reverently. 'Been watching football a good few years, and I surely don't believe I've ever seen any better.'

Once again Jimmy Marvin found his cheeks flushing, but this time it was with delight.

The kick went over and Elmstead Victors were only two points behind the Bromley Bears, nine points to seven. And most of the third quarter and all of the fourth quarter were left.

The rest of the game was lit up by some more great runs by Jimmy and by some great defensive tackling from both teams. But it was darkened by endless fumbles, mistakes, missed field goals and interceptions. As the fourth quarter ground remorselessly on, inexperience, tension and tiredness all conspired together to stall any further scoring.

It began to drizzle again and Jimmy's worn boots made it difficult for him to keep a footing on the greasy turf.

Elmstead used up their last time-out of the game with less than a minute remaining. They were held on the Bromley forty-five yard line. They'd used up three of their four downs and now faced a fourth and twelve situation. It was beyond Paul Allen's most optimistic field goal range. Jimmy and Hebron, both exhausted, stood by their coach, listening to his instructions.

'Send the receivers downfield like we're going to try a last desperate Hail Mary pass. But fake it and slip the ball to Jimmy. Their pass coverage is too good but they aren't happy against the run. They'll lie deep so you can have around twenty yards to pick up some speed, Jimmy. Just go for it, son. Big last run.'

'Sure,' said Jimmy.

Jerry Meredith was a great tactician and his call was perfect. The fake worked and Jimmy took the hand-off from Hebron, sprinting off, drawing on his last flagging reserves of energy.

He wriggled in his orange plastic seat, hardly able to watch, even though he knew what was going to happen.

As he set off there was an almost eerie silence from the spectators, knowing that this was going to be the last play of the final. Elmstead would score, or Bromley would get the ball back and then simply run out the clock.

Everything.

Or nothing.

The young student who'd been operating the camera had also realised that this was the climax of the game – of the whole season. She'd used the slow-motion again, Jimmy thundering up the field, legs driving, a ferocious determination carved on his face. The soundtrack faded down until the only noise, magnified, was a rasping, panting fight for breath.

'Go on, Jim,' said someone in the viewing-room, very quietly.

He dodged at least four tackles, clawing his way to the ten yard line, near the edge of the field, readying himself for the final cut back inside to beat the last defender. But the pitch there was very muddy. His worn studs slipped and he began to fall, losing balance, but still fighting for the end-zone. He hit the turf with his knees and then his shoulders, missing the touchdown by less than two yards.

That was the end of the game. Of the season. Very soon it would be the end of life in England.

8

Over the next couple of days Jimmy found himself feeling really dejected. The cool damp weather persisted, with overcast skies and an easterly wind. Kate had a huge row with Roger over her emigrating, which resulted in yelling and doors slamming. He'd been round the next evening with a bunch of flowers to try and make it up, but Jimmy's sister sent him packing with a flea in his ear.

'Be glad when we've gone,' she'd said, tearfully, that night.

It seemed like everyone in the family was feeling the same.

Mum and Dad went to a farewell party given by her teacher friends. They came home a little bit the worse for drink and Jimmy and Chris could hear them talking animatedly, long after midnight. They both caught Dad saying, on the landing: 'Well, it's too late for that now, love. A darned sight too late for any second thoughts.'

All of the family possessions had been packed away into one huge sort of container, collected by a removal firm. It contained most of their clothes, the music centre, books and a few of their personal things. In the end, the case wasn't more than about half full.

For their last few days, everyone lived a strange existence, floating in an odd limbo. The house was virtually empty and they had to wear the same clothes all the time. Luckily, Mum hadn't packed the family's roll-on deodorant.

With the rotten weather and deprived even of their few records, Jimmy and Chris got on their parents' nerves.

And they got on Kate's nerves.

But most of all they managed to constantly get on each other's nerves.

In the end, Dad called them together in the kitchen, where he was fixing supper. As he talked, he mashed up some fish with lemon juice and pepper and some thinly sliced tomatoes.

'Listen and listen good. There's only four more days 'fore we fly up, up and away. They aren't goin' to be easy days. Not for any of us. We're all giving up a lot, and I guess I'm giving up less than any of you.'

'Sorry, Dad,' muttered Chris.

'Yeah, sorry,' added Jimmy.

Burge Marvin grinned at his downcast sons. 'I know the weather's rotten. Hell, I've been in England long enough to know that summer's a word that means the rain's not so cold as in winter. But when we get over there it could be real hot. When I spoke to Frank last night he said it was way over ninety and the midges were biting.'

'Sounds great, bro,' said Chris to Jimmy. 'Sunstroke and typhus.'

'Pass me the dill, Chris,' said Dad. 'No! Not the crushed ginger! The feathery stuff. That's it. Now, all I'm asking is you try and keep out from under everyone's feet. 'Specially Mum. Can't you find some gentle game to play? Didn't we used to have a set of Monopoly once?'

'Once, Dad. You bought it from a charity shop and all the Chance cards and half the money was missing from it.'

Jimmy laughed. 'And some dog had chewed up Old Kent Road, Kings Cross and Regent Street.'

'Oh, yeah. In the States the game's based on Atlantic City, in Jersey. Just like in the song 'bout being under the boardwalk. You know?'

'You told us before, Dad,' said Chris.

'I did?'

'You did,' agreed Jimmy.

'Right. Now, where did I put the potato peeler? Anyone seen it?'

'It's on the draining-board,' said Chris, picking it up and handing it to his father.

'Now you can either go and find something to do that keeps you out the way, or you can stay and help by peeling . . .' Burgess Marvin discovered that he was suddenly and miraculously on his own in the small kitchen.

'Tie it a bit tighter.'

'It'll tear.'

74

'It won't.

'It will, Jimmy. It's dead old. The material's more like lace than anything.'

'Maybe if we got some sellotape or something like that?'

'String?' suggested Chris, holding the faded pink towel. It had been Jimmy's idea to try and knot it up into a kind of football shape. But it didn't honestly look very good.

Mum saw it and said that it looked like a bundle of rags, done up ugly. Which she claimed was one of her own mother's sayings.

Kate, reluctantly, had agreed to go out with Roger who'd called round for her at about seven o'clock. They'd walked off together up the road, studiously avoiding brushing shoulders in the doorway. Mum and Dad had also gone out to visit Gran, leaving Jimmy and Chris alone in the echoing house.

'Funny, isn't it?'

'What, Chris?'

'To think a part of our life's ending here in just four days. Goodbye to the peeling wallpaper in our bedroom.'

'And the mould in the corner of the hall.'

'And the gutter that leaks.'

'Windows that don't fit.'

'Heating that's cold.'

Jimmy laughed. 'And cooling that's hot. No. But I know what you mean. I've been seein' some of my old mates walkin' round the streets, and I keep thinking that I'll probably never see them again.' He paused. 'Then I see 'em about ten minutes later going the other way. You know?'

Chris pulled a red comb out of the back pocket of his jeans and held it towards his younger brother as if it were a microphone. 'Tell me, Mr Marvin, what do you think you'll miss most about leaving this country?'

Jimmy put his head on one side. 'I dunno.'

Chris turned to an imaginary camera and shook his head. 'He doesn't know! Hard to believe, isn't it?'

'I know what I'll miss.'

'What?'

'I'll miss sort of knowing who we are. I know all 'bout the bad times and Dad's bad back and not having too much money ... No, not having *any* rotten money, most the time. But, at least we're always the Marvins. We stick together and we get through, somehow. Even you and me get on some of the time. You feel that, Chris?'

His older brother leaned back on his bunk bed, picked up the knotted towel and threw it in the air. 'Yes, I know, Jimmy. But we'll still be the same. America won't change that. The Marvins'll always stick together.

'Sure. Chuck us the towel, bro.'

Chris threw it to him, but it bobbled off the ceiling and fell short, slipping through Jimmy's hands to the floor.

His brother laughed. 'Great catch. Trouble is, kid, you're too short for the big time. What's the latest reading?'

'Four-eight-and-a-quarter.'

'You goin' to take that door with you? Keep check-ing your height on the plane? Be good to arrive at immigration with it.'

'Don't forget that when we get to Vermont we're going to have our own rooms. It's worth going just for that. Get away from you and all your disgusting habits.'

Chris picked up the towel. 'You can talk. Look, while everyone's out, let's go play some ball around the house. I'll start in the kitchen and I've got to get a touchdown against the bathroom door. You've got to get the towel off me and score against the kitchen. All right?'

'All right! Give me some skin.'

The brothers solemnly shook hands before starting their game.

The house rang with shrieks and yells as the boys tussled upstairs and downstairs and even in their sister's chamber, normally sacred to Kate. The towel kept falling apart under the tugging and wrestling and they'd call a time-out while it was re-knotted.

Chris scored first, bullocking his way over Jimmy and running up the stairs to dive full-length along the landing and touch the makeshift ball against the chipped door of the bathroom.

'Wonder score from young English boy, Chris Powerhouse Marvin for the Patriots,' he crowed, spiking the towel. Which landed with a sullen thud on the uncarpeted floor.

'First scores don't count in big matches,' replied Jimmy. 'Watch the Pocket Thunderbolt make his comeback run.'

The smaller boy was good as his word.

Taking the towel and jumping from half-way down the stairs, he vaulted clear over Chris's hands and slammed the ball into the kitchen door to bring the scores level.

Now that both boys knew the strengths and weaknesses of the other the game degenerated into a furious maul, the two of them hanging on to the towel, refusing to part with a scrap of it. They were locked together, surging half-way up the stairs when Jimmy managed to crook a leg around a broken banister and haul them both back into the hall.

'Time out, time out!' panted the bigger boy, sitting down against the living-room door, wiping sweat off his face. 'Look, bro, we're goin' to have to tidy up a bit. Mum and Dad'll be home any time now from Gran's house.'

'Yeah. Guess so. Let's just have five more minutes. I got you on the run, Chris.'

'You what?'

'Come on. Five more.'

'All right.'

There followed a brief argument between them on who should have the frayed remains of the towel. Since possession had been shared when they stopped, they agreed to grab hold of a corner each. Chris tried to snatch an advantage but Jimmy knew his brother and was ready for him.

Once again the nearly empty building echoed to their panting and laughter. Chris succeeded in reaching the very top of the stairs before Jimmy's death-grip around his legs pulled him all the bouncing way to the bottom again.

In the noise and excitement, neither of them heard the rusty squeaking of the front gate opening and closing.

Jimmy was unusually strong for his age and height and he was also very fit. Chris was weakened by too much laughter and slowly, and inexorably, the younger boy fought his way into the hall and towards the kitchen door. Chris made a superhuman effort and wrenched him back, nearer the front of the house.

'Now!' shouted Jimmy, putting all his energy into a last desperate explosion. There was a loud ripping noise and he found himself holding only half of the towel. Chris grinned broadly with the other half dangling limply in his hands. But Jimmy had put so much force into his last attempt that he went spinning away up the hall, roaring with laughter, helplessly out of control. His feet danced on the worn and slippery lino, and the torn shreds of the old towel went flying as he struggled to keep himself upright. But he was going too fast.

Sliding.

And falling, legs going up in the air.

Tumbling on his back, and eventually striking the bottom of the frame to the kitchen door. It was a dreadful, jarring blow, and Jimmy heard a weird sound. Like when you walked through a wood and set your heel to a thick, dry twig. There was a stabbing lance of bright fire at the top of his shoulder, where he'd hit.

'You all right, bro?' called Chris, from the other end of the narrow hallway. 'Jimmy?'

'Yeah. Just banged my shoulder.' He stood up, feeling peculiarly wobbly. 'Ow, I don't . . .' The hall was swaying about him and he suddenly began to be aware of wanting to be sick. He tried to lift his right hand to his head, but there was a funny grating noise in his shoulder and he found that he couldn't. The light was coming and going and Chris's voice was distorted and a very long way off. Jimmy blinked, but the hall still looked like he was viewing it from under water.

The kitchen door opened and Jimmy's father just managed to catch his younger son as the boy slumped down in a dead faint.

9

Jerry Meredith sipped at his black coffee. Hot enough and strong enough to float a horseshoe, as he always described it. He had his Eagles cap still perched jauntily on top of the silver-grey curls, his bright eyes looking at the boy sitting in the armchair opposite.

The coach had come around to say his goodbyes to his star player on the morning before the Marvin family left for Vermont. And to commiserate with him on his injury.

'I didn't do that too often. Mebbe three times. Yeah. Broke my ankle twice, leg once, wrist twice, arm three times. I dislocated my shoulder a coupl'a times and my elbow once. Boy, but that was a painful one. Put my thumb out of place once or twice and had some problems with knee ligaments and tendons. Collar-bone's about the weakest part of your body if'n you play football or rugby. Takes a pounding.'

'Specially if you try and knock a door down with your shoulder,' added Jimmy's mother, standing, arms folded, looking out of the front window at the drizzling rain.

Jimmy was half-lying on the sofa, one foot on the floor. He still didn't feel very well and his shoulder was supported in a sling. When he went to bed at night the broken collar-bone was kept snug in a tight figure-of-eight bangage that held his arm against his chest. The doctor had only left a quarter-of-an-hour before Coach Meredith arrived, and found that the boy had a slight temperature.

'Keep him quiet as possible, Mrs Marvin,' he'd urged. 'Don't want him getting so poorly that the airline won't take him.'

Jimmy was despondent. Some of his mates from the team had arranged for them all to meet up in a fast-food joint in Lewisham for a goodbye blow-out. Now he couldn't go and the rotten weather meant they wouldn't be coming up to see him. It was the most miserable ending to life in England.

At least Jerry had come.

'Good coffee, Ma'am,' said the elderly American. 'You'll do fine in New England if'n you give folks a brew like this.'

'The restaurant will be doing entirely traditional English food. We can't decide whether to serve tea or coffee.'

'Both, Mrs Marvin, if you'll take my advice. Not many Americans take kindly to ending a meal without a mug of java.'

'That's what Burge thought.'

'And how's the Mighty Acorn feeling today?'

Jimmy just about managed a smile. 'All right, Coach. Least it didn't happen during the season.'

'True. But soon as you get there and start school you'll have the pigskin under your arm and be running in the touchdowns.'

'Hope so.'

'You'll start in the eighth grade in Junior High, won't you?'

'Yeah. Chris'll be a freshman in High School. Or maybe a second year. We aren't sure.'

'Sophomore,' corrected Jerry. 'That's what they call second years. Depends on his birthday, I guess, where they put him. He could do real well at gridiron with his height and build.'

Jimmy felt cast down by the inference that he wouldn't because he wasn't tall enough. 'I'm still growing,' he said.

'Sure you are. I figure you'll top five feet by the end of the year. But listen, son,' leaning forward and dropping his voice. 'It ain't bigness. You know that better'n me. It's heart, Jimmy, and you got the best and the biggest.'

Jimmy's temperature carried on rising, making him feel both irritable and tired. He was hardly awake when Gran came round for her tearful goodbye to the family.

Chris had been allowed out with his own friends and he still hadn't come back by eleven-thirty. By then both Mum and Dad had gone to bed and Jimmy was lying in his bunk, dozing fitfully. The door inched open and a narrow crack of light speared across the room.

'Chris?'

'No. It's Kate. He not back in yet? Hope he hasn't gone and got himself drunk.'

83

'You all right?'

'Why?'

'Your voice sounds a bit funny. Sort of hoarse. You sure you're all right?' he whispered.

'Sort of. Hey, I saw a couple of your mates from the team.'

'Who?'

'Hebron and what's his name? Tony. They asked how you were and what time we were leaving in the morning. So I told them about ten o'clock.'

'Oh.' Jimmy had been deeply disappointed that he hadn't been well enough to see his friends one last time. Kate still stood in the doorway.

'I'll go to bed, I suppose,' she said.

'You sure you're . . . you know?'

'I've just seen Roger.'

'Oh,' said Jimmy, trying to sit up, but finding the tight bandage around his shoulder and arm made it too difficult. The doctor had said that collar-bones broke easily. But they also healed pretty quickly.

'He tried to persuade me to stay with him. Get engaged and move into a flat together. He's got a new job. We could live in Sidcup. It's nice down there. That's what he said he wanted. He got real upset, Jimmy. Really.'

His sister was on the ragged edge of tears. 'Sssh. You'll wake Mum an' Dad. Come in and shut the door, Kate.'

His sister pushed the bedroom door shut and came and sat on the side of the bed. Jimmy could smell cigarette smoke on her clothes.

'Rog's all right, isn't he?'

'Oh, sure. Roger's all right, Jimmy. Dead nice. Never nasty to me, and he says he loves me. He was crying tonight. We had to leave the pub he was so upset. Made me start off blubbing as well. But . . .'

Jimmy patted her on the back with his good left hand. 'It'll be all right, sis.'

'But, what should I do? Come to Vermont and start all over? Or stay and get married to good old Roger and live in Sidcup?'

'Easy.'

In the dim light of the room, he saw her turn round and look at him, half-smiling. 'Easy, Jim? How d'you make that out?'

'You just do what *you* want. It's not something that's anyone else's business, is it?'

'No. I suppose not, Jimmy. I guess . . . I'm just not really ready for Sidcup. Not yet.'

She leaned across and kissed him on the cheek. He kissed her back, tasting salt tears on her face, the smell of smoke even stronger.

'Better get to bed,' she said. 'Sorry I woke you up, Jim.'

'Wasn't asleep.'

'Want an aspirin?'

'No, thanks. I've had a couple. Feel quite sleepy. But it's like the night before Christmas, isn't it? Know what I mean.'

She nodded, standing and walking quietly to the door. Opening it she hesitated for a moment, silhouetted against the landing light, 'You're a good kid,

Jimmy. Well, some of the time you are. Thanks. Good night, bro.'

'Night, sis.'

'That's it,' said Burgess Marvin, standing in the hall. The minicab had arrived to take them to Heathrow Airport. A last extravagance. The house was quite empty already with that unmistakable feeling of somewhere that wasn't a home any longer.

Jimmy and Chris were in the kitchen. The older boy was nursing a bad head from his farewell party. He hadn't got in until nearly two in the morning and Jimmy had heard him trying to be sick quietly. Never the easiest thing to do. 'Be glad when we get there,' he said. 'This place gives me the creeps. It's like a stone-cold tomb now. Least when we get to the States we'll have a few of our own things there.'

'I've missed my Motown album most,' said Jimmy. 'All the golden oldies from The Supremes and the Four Tops.'

Mum came in then, clutching her hand-bag. She was smiling as she looked around the kitchen. 'Can't say I'm sorry, kids. I wondered how I'd feel about this moment. Now that it's come, I'm delighted. Whatever's over there . . . it can't be as bad as this. And we'll all be together. It'll be good.'

'Come on, Beth,' said Dad, joining them. 'Kate's already in the cab. Everyone ready? Jimmy? You look like you lost a pound and found a penny.' He laughed. 'Taken me all these years to stop saying dollar and cents and now I gotta go back.'

86

'I'm just fed up about feeling rotten and not being able to see any of my mates like Chris did. I'll never . . .'

'Doesn't he know 'bout . . .?' began Dad, shutting his mouth like a steel trap when he caught the look his wife threw him. 'Sorry, love,' he muttered, puzzling his youngest son. Who was also baffled by Chris's broad, cheesey grin.

'Right. No more time. Goodbye house. And good riddance to you,' said Dad, hefting his shoulder bag, leading the way along the hall and out of the front door. Followed by their mother with Chris at her heels. Jimmy was the last one out and Dad shouted back for him to make sure he slammed the front door properly, which he did.

Only then did he turn around and look across the narrow front garden, to where the cab was waiting in the road.

Jimmy shook his head in disbelief. There were about thirty boys there, all of them wearing the navy blue and maroon playing shirts of the Elmstead Victors. In front of them was Jerry Meredith, holding a neatly-wrapped parcel.

'Didn't think we'd let you go without a goodbye, did you, son,' he said.

'I didn't . . .' mumbled Jimmy, seeing from the faces of his family that he'd been shut out from an amazingly well-kept secret.

'Just a small present to carry to your new home,' said Jerry, handing over the parcel. 'Had a whip-round and bought you some new boots. Good cleats

87

on 'em, so you don't slip over in big matches.' His smile defused the teasing words. 'Oh, and there's a playing-shirt from the Victors in there as well. Your own number to remind you of your humble roots when you get to the NFL and become a star.'

Jimmy stood there, holding the damp paper parcel, words clogging up in his throat. Standing and moving made his shoulder hurt and he really wanted to sit down – preferably on his own for a bit.

'What d'you say?' prompted his mother, from the edge of the pavement.

'Oh, thanks, Coach. Thanks a lot. Thanks all of you. I guess . . . I suppose I'll never forget playing with you lot. It was great. Thanks.'

But it still wasn't over. Not quite.

Coach Meredith turned away from him to face the half-circle of boys. Lifting his hand and humming a note, holding it a moment, then dropping his hand. Jimmy thought that he looked like a conductor at the Last Night Of The Proms.

Which wasn't far wrong.

Hebron, who had a great singing voice started it:

'When you feel you can't go on. . . .'

The rest of them joined in, with a superbly rehearsed version of one of Jimmy's all-time favourite songs by the Four Tops. It was just like the TV commercials for Budweiser a couple of years ago, with everyone starting to sing.

'Reach Out, I'll Be There.'

The words of love and support rang out, loud and confident in the morning stillness. People came and stood in their front doors to listen, and the milkman paused with bottles in his hands, a nostalgic smile on his face.

Dad beckoned to his son to join them in the taxi, as the song neared its ending. As he settled himself in the front seat Jimmy thought he would burst with the tangled mixture of emotions.

Just twelve hours later their plane was swooping in to land at Logan International Airport in Boston, Massachusetts.

10

Jimmy's temperature continued to climb during the journey across the Atlantic. One of the stewardesses checked it when they were starting their circling descent over the water towards Boston, reporting it was nearly one-hundred-and-two and that 'the little boy could sure use an aspirin.'

He felt lousy. His shoulder ached and the bandage felt uncomfortably tight after seven hours in the same seat. The food had been rotten. Chris had whispered to him that the tray and the cutlery looked more appetising than the actual meal. During the film, Jimmy had dozed off, waking with a start in time to see Meryl Streep laughing and the end credits rolling up the screen.

As soon as they got off the plane they all felt the heat.

'Phew, what a scorcher!' said Mum. She was wearing a black and white t-shirt with a picture of Robert De Niro on it and looked cool and fresh. Dad seemed nervous at the prospect of meeting his older brother again. Kate had taken some pills to stop her being airsick, and was wandering along with the others in a kind of a daze. Chris had been deputed to keep an eye on Jimmy and was carrying his shoulder-bag for him.

It took for ever for them to get through immigration. Dad asked if Jimmy could go through as he was feeling sick, but the officials were very strict and insisted that all of the paperwork had to be completed before any of them could pass the barriers.

At least all their suitcases had arrived, rolling endlessly round and round the baggage carousel. Customs went quickly and they made their way through to where their relatives were due to meet up with them.

'How'll we find them in this crowd?' asked Jimmy, looking out into a sea of eager faces.

'There,' said Chris, pointing.

It looked like an old bed-sheet, strung out across the railing, with the message painted on it in screaming crimson:

'Welcome Burge, Beth, Katy, Chris and Jim!'

The next ten minutes were a blur of babbling and hugging and hand-shaking and faces that came and went. Uncle Frank, with a massive walrus moustache, smelt of expensive aftershave. Aunt Laura, skinny and elegant, wore white jeans with a broad leather belt and a bronze buckle. Cousin Eddy was a year older than Jimmy, but to the disappointment of the English boy, Eddy was around five-feet-six tall. But there was a grudging satisfaction in seeing that he had a rotten complexion. Nests of fiery pimples clustered around his nose and mouth. Angelina was sixteen, ultra-cool behind a tiny pair of sun-glasses. She had a handshake like five fingers of dead trout.

Everyone was sympathetic about Jimmy's broken

collar-bone. Well, everyone except Angelina, who was too busy moaning about a smear of dirt on one of her pale yellow sneakers.

The spectre of jeg-lag was gleefully joining forces with Jimmy's fever, making him feel wobbly on his feet. The noise and chatter surged around him in strange, barely audible fragments. He heard Eddy Marvin mutter something to his father and he was sure he caught the word 'short' in amongst it.

'What'd he say?' he asked.

'Said parking space here was in real short supply, Jimmy. We were lucky to get in at all. Figure the best we can do is set off now and see you safely home and into a warm bed.'

It sounded wonderful.

Mum and Kate went with Laura and Angie in a trim green Honda hatchback. He and Dad and Chris joined Uncle Frank and Eddy in a huge battered Ford station wagon that swayed around corners like a flying mattress.

Jimmy leaned his head against the glass, peering out, trying to concentrate on not being sick. The roads were bumpier than he'd expected and the traffic, as they ploughed north out of Boston, was much heavier.

'How d'you find your way round the city, Frank?' asked Dad. 'It's worse than London.'

His uncle laughed. 'You drive in Boston, you can drive anywhere. It's all the fault of the Brits. They built the original city and we never got around to making it any easier.'

Fortunately, the car had air-conditioning, so the

summer heat was held at bay. But when Uncle Frank wound down his window to shout at another driver who'd cut him up at traffic lights, a great rush of humid heat flooded them.

For much of the long drive to Vermont, Jimmy slept. All along the Interstate with its wonderful bridges and stands of shadowing trees. Every now and then something would wake the boy. A horn on a car or a stop at a toll-booth or a burst of laughter from the brothers in the front seat.

Late on in the journey, when they were off the busy freeway, he began to glimpse tiny frozen images of rural America. But he was so frayed that he couldn't tell afterwards which were real and which dreamed.

He was sure they passed a sign saying: 'The Biggest Ball Of String In New England . . . Free Coffee and Doughnuts.' But he knew there was something wrong about another billboard for a cafeteria which he *thought* said: 'The eggs we sell tomorrow are still in the cows.'

When they went through somewhere called White River Junction, Eddy nudged him and said: 'Only 'bout 'nother twenty miles, Jimmy. You feelin' all right?'

'Yeah, fine, thanks,' he answered, but if someone had offered him a small blue tablet that would have given him an instant and painless death, Jimmy would have snatched it gratefully. He didn't think he'd ever felt so rotten in his entire life.

His head ached. His stomach was churning and

boiling, making him feel sweating hot one moment and freezing cold the next. His throat was sore and it hurt to swallow. Though he'd had several glasses of Coke on the plane, he was desperately thirsty. But he kept quiet as he didn't want to interrupt the conversation in the front. It was all about the new restaurant, involving credits, federal hygiene and electric ranges.

Commodity values and purchasing forwards at discount. None of it made the least sense to Jimmy.

His damaged shoulder felt almost like the bone had broken again and the splintered ends were rubbing together at every lurch of the car.

The countryside looked beautiful. Rolling hills, many of them covered in all kinds of trees. Jimmy had read up a bit about Vermont and he knew that the spreading forests of maple and oak were one of the wonders of the state. But despite the grandeur of it all, he'd happily have swapped it for his old bunk-bed back home in Hither Green.

'Soon be there!' called Uncle Frank.

'You boys OK in the back?' asked Dad, turning round in his seat, unable to conceal a wince of discomfort at a twinge from his damaged spine. The long, cramped flight over had been purgatory for him and he looked pale and tired.

'Sure, Uncle Burge,' replied Eddy.

Jimmy noticed that Chris had fallen asleep, head lolling from side to side.

'In winter this road gets buried fifteen feet deep in snow,' said Eddy Marvin. 'They plough it regular. You gotta make sure you don't leave nothin' out near

94

the road else the plough'll pick it up and wipe it away. Angie lost a bike that way, coupla years ago. Left it on the lawn when the first fall of snow came and clean forgot it. We found what was left of it a quarter mile down towards the village.'

'Here's North Strafford, guys,' called Francis. 'Your home sweet home. Our store's on the left, with the restaurant next along. House is up a black-top.'

'What's a black-top?' asked Jimmy.

His father answered. 'It's just another name for a road. There's only a couple of others shops . . . I mean, "stores", aren't there, Frank?'

'Most important's the general store, run by Josiah Hedges and his wife, Ginny. You can get anything here from postage stamps to pies. From guns to . . . to gossip. Step easy with Jos and Ginny. They don't take that kindly to outsiders at first, but they're real good folk. And there's the garage and a little place run by Margie Dickinson that sells kids' clothes and stuff like that.'

Now Chris had woken up and he and Jimmy were both staring eagerly from the windows of the car. It was hugely, immeasurably different from their old home. The old home that they'd left barely a dozen hours ago.

'You sure you get plenty of tourists round here, Frank?' asked Dad, unable to conceal the worry in his voice.

'You seen my turnover figures on the curios business, Burge. From spring through the fall we get plenty of visitors. New Yorkers who want some

95

weekend rural peace. And in winter there's plenty of good skiing not far from here.'

'Skiing?' said Chris. 'Honest? I always wanted to try that. I'd have loved to have gone on one of the school trips to Austria but we couldn't ever find the . . .'

'Money,' finished Dad. 'You know you don't have to worry 'bout sayin' it, son. Let's just hope you won't have to say it much longer.'

'Here it is,' said Frank, slowing the car to a crawl. One of the things that Jimmy had noticed immediately they left Boston was how much quieter the roads were. Here, in this beautiful land of rolling hills and woods, you only seemed to pass another car every half hour or so.

'Bygones Are Bygones' said the main sign, in an ornamented, Gothic kind of golden lettering. Under it a smaller sign said 'Buygones are Bargains'.

The window was crowded with bits of glass and china and some furniture could dimly be seen further back in the interior. But the sunlight bouncing off the plate-glass made it hard to make anything out properly.

It was the building next door that held all their eyes.

Jimmy was conscious of the Honda pulling up behind them with Mum and Kate in it. Uncle Frank switched off the engine and there was a sudden silence.

'Course we'll all walk down and have a good look round tomorrow,' he said. 'Know what jet-lag's like.

And with Jimmy's shoulder and all that. . . . But there it is. What d'you think, brother?'

Burgess Marvin took a long time to reply, which both Jimmy and Chris knew was generally a sign that he wasn't very happy. Finally: 'Looks like there's a lot to do, Frank.'

Uncle Frank laughed and clapped his hands. 'Terrific! Hear that Eddy? Your Uncle Burge's gotten the Brit habit of understatement! Course there's a lot to do, Burge. Lots and lots. But you gotta see past what's there to what's goin' to be there. The structure's sound as a bell.'

The building was joined to the antique store and looked roughly the same size. But Jimmy could see that it actually went quite a bit further back to where he guessed the kitchens must be. The painted sign over the door was so faded and peeling that it was illegible. All that could be read was a message scrawled in white finger-paint inside the left-hand window, with some letters reversed.

'Close Down. Thanks To All Custumurs.'

'Short and sweet,' muttered Chris.

'Sure is dirty, Frank,' said Dad, 'but I guess I figured it would be. You're sure there's not zoning problems or health and hygiene?'

'Nope. Spoken to everyone. They'll be happy as china rabbits if'n we can make a go of this. Good for North Strafford is good for Vermont. Good for Vermont is good for everyone.'

'Yeah,' said Jimmy's father. 'Guess I'm just bone-tired, Frank. Don't mean to be a party-pooper and put it all down. God knows I want it to succeed and I'm goin' to work for that. Let's go and see the house and get Jim to bed. Get us all to bed, and start fresh after breakfast tomorrow.'

Frank Marvin leaned across the wide front seat and hugged his younger brother. Grinning from ear to ear as he looked at the boys in the rear of the big wagon. 'Let's go, team, huh?'

Jimmy was feeling so rough again that he could hardly even raise a smile.

They'd seen a polaroid photo of their house, but it hadn't done it justice.

'All of it?' said Kate.

'Sure,' said her aunt, putting her arm around the girl. 'All yours. Cellar and attic and garden. Whole darned shooting-match.'

It was a wooden frame house in a half acre of land, bordering on the road on one side, and on woods on the other three sides. It had been built around 1887, at a time that the village was beginning to grow and thrive. Painted white it had a porch along the front of the ground floor. 'First floor we call it over here, Jimmy,' reminded Uncle Frank. There was a matching balcony on the top floor. The doors and windows all had fine-mesh screens screwed down over them. To keep out the midges, Eddy explained.

The furniture was very basic; mainly heavy wooden pieces, but solid and serviceable. Uncle Frank said he'd had a message that their possessions would be delivered within the next forty-eight hours. Then it would begin to look like their own home. Mum and Aunt Laura went together into the kitchen. Eddy and Angelina drifted away to go back to their own house, a quarter mile up the road. 'Up the black-top,' thought Jimmy to himself. He and his brother and sister were far more interested in upstairs.

The bedrooms.

Dad had shouted up that he and Mum were having the main room at the front that overlooked the long balcony. There were three other rooms, one at each side of the house and one at the back. They were all more or less the same size and shape, with more or less the same kind of view.

'I like this one with the big mirror,' said Kate, standing possessively in front of it.

'I like the one this side,' called Chris. 'Got a big walk-in cupboard. I mean "closet". I'll never learn the language.'

'What 'bout you, Jimmy?' shouted Kate. 'How d'you feel about the room at the rear?'

He didn't answer. They'd *arrived*! They'd gone and done it now. Up with the roots and over the ocean to this strange and beautiful country.

The room was eleven feet square. Wood panelled to about waist-height, then decorated in faded wall-paper in a faint blue stripe. There was a large wardrobe against one wall. Desk under the window. Table at the head of the bed. Some shelves on the other side wall. There was only one picture in the bedroom. A small framed etching of a young boy in medieval clothes.

The view was across the patch of lawn, past a rusting swing. The ground dropped sharply and the boy could hear the far-off chattering and sound of water over stones. Beyond that was the beginning of the woods, spreading away and away into the distance.

The bed was much larger than an ordinary single size; very nearly as big as Jimmy's parents' bed had been back in England. It was covered in an old patchwork quilt, made from hundreds of triangular pieces of cloth. He thought it looked the most comfortable bed that he'd ever seen.

Across the landing he could hear Kate and Chris, comparing views from windows. Downstairs someone had put on a brew of fresh coffee, the scent floating up the staircase.

Jimmy thought he'd lie on the bed, just for a couple of minutes.

And maybe close his eyes . . .

11 Jimmy Marvin didn't wake up until three o'clock the following afternoon. His temperature had slunk back to normal, his shoulder felt vastly better and he was ready to go and face the new world.

But first he felt in need of a bath. He pulled on his jeans and t-shirt and padded barefooted across the floor of his room. *His* room. Just as he was about to walk out on to the landing, his eye was caught by something.

There was some kind of mark on the edge of the bedroom door. He stopped and peered at it. Though much of the house had been decorated, it was still possible to see a number of tiny scratches. With a thrill of delight, the English boy recognised what they were. There was no way of knowing how old the marks were, but some time in the last hundred years a boy who'd lived in that room had measured his height against the door. Just like Jimmy had done back in England.

Before going to have his bath, he slipped downstairs and borrowed a knife. Cutting a tiny nick to mark the precise level of his own height. With a private thrill of excitement, he saw that his scratch was within a fraction of an inch of the highest previous mark on the door.

Somehow that made Jimmy feel more at home.

There was only a week from their arrival to the opening of the new school term. Or 'semester' as Uncle Frank reminded them.

Jimmy visited the local doctor who checked out his collar-bone and told him that it was healing well. He was allowed to take the figure-of-eight bandage off during the day, providing that he was careful. Just wearing it for another few nights to make sure he didn't accidentally hinder the mending process while he was sleeping.

The nearest small town, Porchester, was where both their schools were. The Thomas Melville Junior High for Jimmy, and the Lynette Howell High School just a couple of blocks further down Main Street, where Chris would be starting.

Both boys were nervous, but Eddy and Angelina had been extremely friendly and helpful. Going in with them on the twice-a-day bus, showing them around Porchester. They took them to the best fast-food eateries, the town's ice-cream parlour, a large bookshop and a record store that sold discounted albums.

They also introduced them to some of their own friends. Both Jimmy and Chris were amazed at how easily they were adopted into the groups. Within the week most of their initial fears had vanished.

Jimmy had had a problem with two boys who he learned might be in his class. Both played for the school gridiron team.

Fortunately they were both a year ahead of him in class, but they went out of their way to tease him over his accent and his lack of knowledge of life in America. And they patted him on the head and told him he was a 'real cute little guy'. One of them even said he'd like to tie a pretty ribbon around Jimmy's waist and dangle him from the handlebars of his BMX trail bike.

Dad had warned all three of his children that they would get a certain amount of hassling. 'Hazing' was what he called it. But his advice, drummed into them with utmost seriousness, was to ride with it. If you let them have their laughs and got on with life, it wouldn't take long for them to get bored and find a new source of amusement.

Because of his height and size, Chris didn't have any problems.

Because of *his* height and size, Jimmy did get some teasing.

But his own natural sense of humour, coupled with his considerable knowledge of the gridiron game, enabled the boy to follow his father's advice and ride it all. When they kidded him about his lack of inches, he replied with his own exaggerated jokes about the advantages of being small:

'Not so far to fall when I get hit. I can walk under most turnstiles. Dogs and old ladies love me. I don't have to bend down to tie the laces on my boots. I duck under most tackles. I save time by not having to open doors . . . I just walk clean under them.'

And many more.

After a couple of days the teasing began to fade

away and the English kid was cheerfully adopted into the school and village groups.

Jimmy's injured shoulder meant that he wasn't able to take any part in the Junior High sports programme for a fortnight. When the final restraining bandage was thrown away he began to exercise again. The black-top where their house stood was a quiet country back road. If they saw three vehicles a day going along it they figured something must be wrong. The two boys were therefore able to go out and throw a football that Uncle Frank had bought for them in Porchester. As a running back, Jimmy didn't have too great a need of either catching or throwing skills, but it was his ambition to be a really fine all-round football player.

His chief concern was to rebuild his fitness. The last couple of weeks in England and the first two weeks in Vermont had given him little chance to work on his speed-training and his stamina. Using the side of the lane, he walked and ran and sprinted, pushing himself as hard as he could, finding that his speed over the first forty yards – which is the most important distance for an American footballer – was unimpaired. Indeed, in the clean, green country air he began to feel better and fitter than he ever had.

Jimmy couldn't wait to get back on the field and start carrying the football for real again.

Apart from the boys starting at their schools, the most important thing that dominated the life of the whole family was starting to get The Olde Roaste Beefe ready for its opening date at the end of September. They wanted to take advantage of the huge influx of tourists coming to the region to admire the fiery splendour of the New England autumn. Or 'fall' as they called it.

Burge Marvin's feelings were like a roller-coaster. When he was planning the menus and immersing himself in the wondrous arts of cooking, he was on a high, licking his lips in delight at the opportunity to turn his hobby into dollars.

But in the late afternoons, when they were all down there, cleaning and painting, he'd be plunged into a morass of misery.

'Why have we done this, Beth? This is madness. Nobody'll come all the way out here just to eat beef and Yorkshire pudding. Or lamb and mint sauce. Or rabbit with redcurrants. It's filthy and cramped and we've given up life in England for this.'

'Well, Burgess Marvin,' said Mum. 'I never thought I married such a wimp.'

'What?'

'Someone who wants to give up before they've even started. And who has the nerve to talk to me about "life" in England.'

'But look at it,' gesturing to what was to become the main dining-room of their restaurant. 'Half decorated and a quarter ready.'

Jimmy interrupted, pointing around with a brush that dripped pale green paint: 'But next week it'll be three-quarters decorated and well over half ready. Won't it?'

Both parents laughed, Dad shaking his head. 'Not if I stand here moaning all the time it won't, son. Let's get to it.'

Chris went along to the first Saturday training for his High School football team. Jimmy accompanied him, hitching a lift in with Uncle Frank.

There were quite a few boys there that they both knew, including the two lads who'd teased Jimmy about his height. The older brother of one of them, Keith Sheldon, was the back-up quarterback for the Lynette Howell High School and he burst out laughing when Jimmy and Chris arrived.

'Tall and Tiny, the Limey Lovelies!' he crowed. 'Battler Brit and his midget brother. Guess we could use you as a mascot, son,' he sneered at Jimmy.

'The last person that said that on a football field ended up with a faceful of dirt,' said Chris to the American teenager.

'Yeah, sure, sure. And you figure to be a linebacker, do you?'

'I try.'

'Well, you try linebackin' 'gainst me this afternoon and see who ends up with a mouthful of dirt.'

The coach of the High School team, a youngish man who walked with a stick, Pete Hays, came over at the tail-end of the conversation.

'Hear you're making the new recruit feel welcome, in your own inimitable way, Keith.'

Sheldon sniffed and shuffled his feet. 'Just kind of . . .'

The coach nodded. 'I know. Well, Keith, let's see who does the dirt-eating. You can play on the starting line-up for a quarter and we'll put Chris here as outside linebacker on the other squad.'

'I'd like that,' said Chris eagerly.

Jimmy wished his brother luck and went off to sit in the deserted stand with a few of the younger boys and a scattering of girls. He had his fingers crossed for his big brother, praying that he'd do well against the loudmouth.

On the first down, Keith fumbled the snap and dropped the ball. On the second down Chris brushed aside his block and tackled the quarterback, hard, from the side. Keith's third attempt at least saw him with the ball snug in his hand. But seeing Chris starting to break towards him he backpedalled furiously and threw a pass that looped way over the side-line.

Chris sacked him again on the next play, even though Keith had retreated into the pocket for protection.

'Havin' a good game, your brother,' said Jimmy, to Bobby Sheldon, one of his earlier tormentors.

'Shut your lip, kid,' replied the American. 'Just beginner's luck for your brother.'

In the next half-hour, Chris's beginner's luck carried on running for him. He sacked Keith Sheldon three more times, forcing the coach to pull him out of the practice.

Although he was only a rookie in the squad, Coach Hays told Chris Marvin that he would be starting at outside linebacker for the High School team in their first game, the following week. Providing he could learn the play-book in time.

Jimmy was playing *Love Is Here And Now You're Gone* by the Supremes, his head-phones turned up loud. The massive case with all the family's possessions had finally turned up and the house was starting to look and feel like home.

On a recommendation from Uncle Frank, Kate Marvin had managed to get a job in the book-store in Porchester. A young man who ran the Poetry and Drama sections of the shop also lived in North Strafford and she was able to get a lift from him each day. That Wednesday he'd asked her out and after some consideration she'd accepted.

The restaurant was looking like it would actually open on time.

Inside it was all decorated, in pale green and cream, with brass lights that Uncle Frank had picked up from a house that was being demolished in nearby Norwich. Which the Marvins had quickly learned wasn't pronounced in the English way. You had to say it as if it were spelled 'Norewitch'.

Although he was a whizz with food and cooking, Dad didn't have much of a head for figures or for planning, which was where his wife came into her own. After years of trying to balance a budget on virtually no income, Beth Marvin found it easy to handle the business side of the restaurant.

After long discussions with Francis and Laura

Marvin, it was agreed, at last, that they'd start casually. They'd just put up the 'Open' sign and then make their mistakes without undue pressure. Then, after a couple of weeks, they could announce a Grand Opening and get the project properly launched.

For some days there'd been the idea floated of having sawdust on the floor and a dartboard. But the English Marvins all gave that the thumbs-down, pointing out that it sounded like a dreadful parody of an English pub.

'It's goin' to be great food and good drink and a friendly feeling,' protested Burge. 'We don't need cheap surface dressing for that.'

He got his way.

'Collar-bone?'

'Yes, Coach.'

'Doctor says you can play?'

'Yes, Coach.'

'Your brother's the big linebacker they're all talkin' 'bout over at the High School?'

'Yes, Coach.'

'And you figure you're a running back, do you, Jimmy? Don't tell me. The answer's goin' go be "Yes, Coach" isn't it?'

Jimmy grinned. 'Yes, Coach. It is.'

'How tall are you, son?'

'Four-foot-nine,' he said, waiting for the usual put-down. But it never came.

'That's all right with me, Jimmy. A well-made and well-aimed bullet can bring down a charging elephant.

You got guts for the run and the tackle and you an' me'll get on real good. You understand me, do you, son?'

'Yes, Coach.'

'Saturday we play against one of the New Hampshire schools just across the state line. The Beulah May Junior High. Last two years they beat us, but three, maybe four, years before that, we licked them. I figure it's our turn again.'

'Yes, Coach.'

'I may put you in and I may not. Long as you do like I ask and give it your best shot, then it'll be all right. See you Saturday, Jimmy.'

'Bye, Coach.'

As he and Chris practised in the warm summer evening, Jimmy recalled his dreams when he'd played back in England. Every time he caught a pass he magically became the world-famous football star, known by his legions of admiring fans as the Pocket Thunderbolt.

The voice from the garden broke into his fantasy. 'Jimmy! You haven't tidied up your room. Come and do it right now.'

'Sure, Mum,' he said.

Friday evening saw Frank and Burge on an urgent last-minute errand, accompanied by Beth and Kate, to collect the table napkins and cloths from the manufacturer at Burlington, a long way off to the west on the shores of the beautiful Lake Champlain. So

Jimmy and Chris went to have supper with Aunt Laura, Eddy and Angie.

Paradoxically, if Burge was one of the best cooks in all Vermont, Aunt Laura slid effortlessly into the worst ten. Jimmy and Chris had always heard the family jokes about her managing to burn a boiled egg and serve fried breakfast cereal under the impression that it was instant potato.

Now they lived close by and had eaten a couple of meals in her house, they realised that the jokes weren't true. If anything they failed to tell the whole, dreadful story.

Aunt Laura served up chicken pieces with baked potatoes and sweet corn, followed by apple pie and vanilla ice-cream. The chicken was pre-cooked. The sweet-corn was from a can. The apple-pie was frozen and the ice-cream was from a huge gallon tub out of the family freezer in their basement.

Not an awful lot to go wrong!

Wrong.

As soon as his knife clashed on tinkling crystals of ice in the middle of the chunk of chicken breast, Jimmy knew that this was going to be one of Aunt Laura's specials.

'I'm real sorry the sweet-corn's gone kind of mushy,' she said.

'Ugh, Mom, it's yellow gunk,' moaned Eddy. 'And my potato's raw an' cold clean through the middle.'

'I think yellow's such a pretty colour,' said Angelina with a pleasantly vacuous and distant smile at the boys.

A few days earlier Jimmy had 'accidentally' overheard a conversation between his parents about their American cousins. Dad had said that Angie was 'nice enough but a real air-head. Pure ear-to-ear oxygen.'

The more he saw of the teenager, the more Jimmy saw what his father had meant.

Laura had forgotten to take the ice-cream out of the freezer so it bent the spoon when they tried to scoop it from the tub. Jimmy had offered to keep an eye on heating the apple pie in the big gleaming oven. It was the only part of the meal that tasted all right.

'Frank said you were keen on cooking as well, Jimmy,' said Laura. 'This pie is wonderful. You sure have your father's golden touch with food, don't you?'

'Only had to heat it up,' he mumbled.

'Oh, but it's terrific, Jim,' sighed Angie. 'Just sort of melts in the mouth. You're a genius.'

Though it sounded like the girl was being sarcastic, Jimmy decided that she wasn't. That was just her way of talking.

Eddy grinned. 'Yeah. For once we got apple pie like Mom *don't* make. Thanks, Jimmy.'

After the meal the boys talked about their plans to go and watch the Red Sox playing at Fenway Park, Boston's huge baseball ground.

Angelina had gone off to her room where she would curl up on her bed and chatter endlessly on the phone to her friends.

Jimmy, Chris and Eddy then sat down to watch the movie on the television. It was one of the English boys' favourites. 'Stand By Me', based on the Stephen

King novella about four young boys growing up in a small town. There's a lovely sequence in it that was one of Jimmy's best-liked bits. The boys are sitting around discussing important matters, like what kind of a creature is Goofy? They agree Mickey is a mouse, Donald a duck and Pluto a dog. But *what* is Goofy?

As they walked back together through the quiet, moonlit evening, the brothers were laughing about their supper and their relations. They both agreed that the American branch of the Marvin family seemed really nice.

'Think you're goin' to like it over here in Vermont?' asked Chris.

Jimmy sidefooted a pebble out of the path. 'Guess so, bro? How 'bout you?'

Chris's teeth flashed white in the silver light of the moon. 'Like the man who fell off the thirty storey office building. Folks all the way down heard him calling: "So far, so good. So far, so good."'

The old joke made both of them laugh. It wasn't until they were very nearly home that Jimmy realised that tomorrow was the big day for him. His first try-out for the football team of the Junior High.

12

There was a good luck card propped up against his coffee mug when Jimmy came down for breakfast the next morning. It showed a beefy American footballer, steam snorting from his nostrils, pawing at the ground like a charging bull. The caption simply said: 'Try For It'.

Everyone had signed it, including Frank, Laura and their two children, with a variety of good lucks and best wishes. Mum had written along the bottom: 'Sorry we can't be there, son. But tonight's the night for the Olde Roaste Beefe. Just do your best. We'll all be thinking about you.'

The butterflies were busy in Jimmy's stomach as he finished getting changed. Even the biggest of games home in England only attracted a few dozen parents and supporters. When he'd arrived at the ground, given a lift by the father of one of the other North Strafford boys in the team, he'd been amazed to see literally hundreds of men, women and children streaming into the rows of bench seats.

'Is it always like this?' he asked the team's kick return specialist, David Locke.

'No. Big matches later in the season . . . specially

if'n we get to any area finals . . . you get some real big crowds.'

The butterflies multiplied and changed themselves into crawling lizards. Between arriving and going out on the field, Jimmy found it necessary to pay three visits to the toilet.

The Coach was waiting for them out on the side of the field. Standing only a couple of inches below six feet, and wearing a New England Patriots satin jacket over playing pants. Carrying a clipboard in the right hand, staring around over half-moon glasses with silver frames.

Her name was Christine O'Keefe.

On their first meeting she'd given Jimmy a firm handshake and introduced herself. 'You know that my name's Christine O'Keefe. I've been coach of the Thomas Melville Junior High School for twenty-two years. If we meet socially then you may call me Miss O'Keefe. The rest of the time you will call me "Coach" and nothing else. Forget that and you'll get a size nine sneaker where the sun doesn't shine. Is that clear, Jimmy Marvin?'

'Yes, Coach,' he'd replied.

'Beulah May Junior High are a load of pussy-cats. I believe that you are, in general, larger and faster and better than them. I would be disappointed if I were to be proven wrong.'

Jimmy had never met a coach like Miss O'Keefe. She was amazingly thorough and very knowledgeable

115

and some of her play-calls were brilliant. Jimmy just hoped he didn't disappoint her.

The Beulah May team kicked off to start the game. David Locke, the home kick return, was standing rubbing his hands together. Catching Jimmy glancing at him, he winked. 'Run me some good blocks, man,' he called.

The kick was short and slant, bouncing once and lurching awkwardly in the air. But David Locke was there, picking it up cleanly and starting his run up the field. Jimmy's function on the play was to run ahead of him and try and block out any would-be tacklers. There was a huge defender, rushing toward him and Jimmy picked his moment to dive at his legs, but the boy was so big and Jimmy was so nervous, that the block was badly mistimed and the opposing player ran over him and ploughed into David Locke, mowing him down before he'd had time to really get into his stride.

Winded and aware of his mistake, Jimmy lay there, not wanting to get up. He knew that there'd been a fraction of a second's hesitation because of his broken collar-bone, and it worried him. A hand grabbed him and hauled him to his feet and he blinked his eyes open to stare into the face of Coach O'Keefe.

'Bad luck, son. Good try, though. You'll get him next down.' Jimmy nodded and took a couple of deep breaths. 'You know what I heard about broken bones, Jimmy?'

'No, Coach.'

'They heal stronger than they were before. You ever heard that?'

'Yeah, Coach. I have.'

The woman nodded. 'Fine.' Then raising her voice she said: 'Let's go, team!'

The skinny wide receiver, Hunter Goldblum, patted Jimmy on the back as the offence took up their positions. 'Don't worry, Jim, my man,' he said. 'You gotta break some eggs 'fore you get to make an omelette.'

Jimmy still felt a bit shaken and didn't get on the field for the next series of plays: a strong drive from their own twelve, generalled by the black quarterback, Eric Wood. Several times he hit the Junior High's massive tight end, Bret Dillon, who broke tackles and ran over defenders like a smaller version of the New York Giants' player, Mark Bavaro.

On a second and ten call at the Beulah May fifteen yard line, Eric Wood hit Hunter Goldblum for nine yards. Bringing a third and one on the six yard line. The noise from the spectators was louder than anything that Jimmy Marvin had ever heard. Coach O'Keefe called him to her. 'This is right team blue, Jimmy. You know it?'

'Sure. Ball to the tail back, Number Twenty-Nine. Can't remember his name, though.'

'Declan. Good. Now, see the big ox in the middle of their defence? Middle linebacker?'

'Sure. Been watching him all afternoon.'

'Name's Rusty Nelson. Hits like Samurai Singletary. He's waitin' to come over the top and hit Declan and knock him into the middle of next week. All you have to do is go in first and block him and then Declan can make the down behind you.'

'Just like that?' said Jimmy, with a grin. 'Sure, Coach. Whatever you say.'

As Jimmy came on the field he caught a ferocious glance from Nelson, who obviously guessed why he was being brought in.

The offence took up their positions. Jimmy lined up a few steps back from Eric and five yards in front of Declan. He already knew how good the boy was at all sports. He was the New England hurdles champion in his age group.

Eric barked out the call. Jimmy couldn't take his eyes off the big boy in the Beulah May colours of gold and green. His friends had been talking about Rusty Nelson before the kick-off. Hunter had said that he was 'mean as a junk-yard dog', and Jimmy believed it. The linebacker's chiselled face broke into a grin under the scraped and battered helmet. A grin that said 'ready or not, kid' to Jimmy.

The ball was in the hands of the quarterback, who faked a pass to Jimmy. Powering himself forwards, he cradled his hands to his chest, as though he'd taken the pass, drawing some of the defensive players out of position. Behind him, Declan had taken the ball and was readying himself for take-off.

Rusty Nelson wasn't fooled by the feint and he moved forwards on the far side of the scrimmage. As Declan made his jump, the linebacker leaped to meet him and send him backwards. At the same moment, a flying Number Twenty-Six emerged and drove his shoulder into the big teenager's chest. Nelson sprawled sideways, arms wide in surprise, leaving a gap the size of a barn wall. Declan high-stepped over the carnage that Jimmy had caused, through the hole. Not just for a first down, but all the way into the unguarded end-zone for a touchdown.

As soon as he'd spiked the ball triumphantly in the turf, the boy ran to Jimmy and they leaped together, slapping palms in the 'high-five'.

'Good,' said Coach O'Keefe to Jimmy. 'Real good, son.'

Throughout the rest of the first and second quarters, Coach O'Keefe kept Jimmy on the field for his blocking skills on both passing and running plays.

By half-time the Thomas Melville Junior High of Porchester, Vermont, was leading by a healthy twenty-eight points to fourteen. Eric had thrown touchdown passes to Bret Dillon, Hunter Goldblum and to Declan.

During the interval Coach O'Keefe called Declan, who was captain on the field, and Jimmy over. 'Two scores a reasonable cushion?' she asked.

'Guess so, Coach,' answered Declan.

'And you reckon to be a running back, Jimmy, don't you?'

'Like the chance, Coach,' he replied, feeling a flutter of excitement.

'You've earned a run, boy,' she said. 'You've

worked for me well these two quarters. Go for it on the first play.'

Jimmy didn't disappoint her.

The first time he took the ball from the quarterback he ran clear over Rusty Nelson, sprinting fifty yards only to be nudged out of bounds on the opponents' twenty, by a despairing free safety's tackle.

But it wasn't to be too long before the young English boy notched up his first Vermont touchdown. He had managed three slashing runs before finally hitting paydirt.

Taking a pass in a second and goal situation, on the three yard line. Seeing a defender hurtling at him, Jimmy dropped his shoulder and whacked him out of the way, feeling the shock of the attempted tackle clear to his toes. Bouncing off and angling through a narrow gap, breaking into the end-zone, still on his feet.

It was like all of his dreams. Dodging lampposts in drizzling South London streets, imagining just such a moment as this.

By the end of the game the Porchester fans were delirious with delight. They hadn't just defeated their old rivals. They'd wiped them clean off the field.

At the beginning of the third quarter Jimmy Marvin ran in another touchdown covering nearly seventy yards to score. Ending the game with one-hundred-and-ninety rushing yards to his credit. Apart from his own scores, he also set up opportunities for his team. Eric Wood hit Hunter Goldblum for two more short range touchdowns, giving victory by a massive fifty-six points to twenty-one.

It was early evening before the celebrations began to ease down. Coach O'Keefe insisted on driving Jimmy home to North Strafford in her own car, along the misty winding roads. She talked excitedly about their win, and how having a running back as good as Jimmy was going to alter her game plans. And give her the promise of a solid, winning season.

'I hear your folks are opening up a restaurant, next to Frank Marvin's gift shop. He's your uncle, isn't he? And I hear it'll be real old English food. Is that right?'

'Yes, Coach,' he replied.

'When are they starting?'

'Sort of tonight.'

'Really. Then I guess I might treat myself to a victory meal, if you think they wouldn't mind it?'

'I'm sure they wouldn't.'

The car rolled towards the crest of the hill that lead down into the village's main street. Now the nervous tension of the game was easing, the boy began to wonder how things were at the Olde Roaste Beefe.

'My goodness!' exclaimed Miss O'Keefe, making the car swerve to the side in her surprise.

There was still enough light left for them to see that the parking lot in front of the restaurant was absolutely packed with vehicles. More cars were up on the sidewalk opposite and there was even a queue by the front door.

After they'd squeezed in further down the street, Jimmy led his Coach to the back door and introduced her to his parents, to Chris and Kate, and to the American branch of the Marvin family.

Everyone was oozing with delight.

They were booked out for the whole night and Kate had been on the phone all afternoon taking reservations, once the word spread they were opening.

'So much for the quiet evening,' said Dad, wiping sweat off his forehead. 'But I'm sure we can fit Miss O'Keefe in somewhere.'

'Sure can, bro,' grinned Uncle Frank. 'Boy, they're happy as china rabbits in there. Can't get enough of the roast beef and Yorkshires.'

Mum and Dad stood either side of Jimmy, their arms proudly around him as Coach O'Keefe recounted the story of the afternoon's win, and their son's rookie triumph.

'Terrific, Jim,' said Mum, beaming at him. 'That's just great.'

'Think he's got the makings, Miss O'Keefe?' asked Dad.

She smiled. 'I don't believe in giving lads nicknames after just one game, Mr Marvin, but I'll make an exception in your boy's case.'

'What's that?' asked Jimmy.

She solemnly shook his hand. 'I'd like to welcome to the team of the Thomas Melville Junior High School, and to Porchester, and to Vermont. And to the United States of America . . .' raising her voice, 'Jimmy Marvin, the Pocket Thunderbolt!'

It was a good moment.